D0323852

WOUNDED MOON

GARY COOK

STOEGER PUBLISHING COMPANY, ACCOKEEK, MARYLAND

WOUNDED MOON

GARY COOK

© 1998 Gary Cook
All rights reserved.

No part of this book may be reproduced or transmitted
in any form or by any means, electronic or mechanical,
including photocopying, recording, or by any information storage and retrieval system, without permission in
writing from the Publisher.

Published 2004 by
Stoeger Publishing Company
17603 Indian Head Highway, Suite 200
Accokeek, Maryland 20607

BK0409
ISBN: 0-88317-272-0
Library of Congress Control Number: 2003106087

All characters, names and incidents in this book are
entirely fictitious and any resemblance to persons living
or dead is purely coincidental.

Distributed to the book trade and
to the sporting goods trade by:
Stoeger Industries
17603 Indian Head Highway, Suite 200
Accokeek, Maryland 20607

Printed in the United States of America.

For Kristen and Kary,
who search for truths and faith to be brave.

*And God shall pour out his spirit upon all flesh
and sons and daughters shall prophesy and young
men will see visions...*

—Joel

PROLOGUE

I am reluctant to give this manuscript to anyone, much less someone with power to pub-
lish. I have worked my entire career in the mountains of eastern Tennessee as a state wildlife officer. That is all I ever wanted. I didn't ask for this.

Staring outside my open window for the better part of an hour, I notice the air is crisp and a blue jay is scolding on the mountain. I hear water rolling over its course in the river behind my cabin, smoothing the rocks over time. If James Taylor were here, he would craft a song about it that would make me want to sing along. But there is only me. I didn't ask for this.

So I write these words from the memory of a woman torn between two realities. It is her story. She lived it. It was beyond my strength to decline her request to write it down. Our meeting was chance, or fate, or destiny, depending on one's theory of life's movements. I now realize how wonderfully connected we are. All of us. Eventually, we must confront her story in our lives, the heart of it anyway. It is inevitable. Even if we didn't ask for it. It began a long, long way from Tennessee. It all started with the bear ...

CHAPTER ONE

*T*he extraction would be difficult, almost insane. The team moved slowly, each member alone with wandering thoughts and the sound of boots in the snow. Doc was cold, the wind stung his face through the hood of his parka and only the fear of something going awry nagged at his brain, or maybe his heart — the fear of being caught. It overpowered the excitement that normally accompanied a research project of this difficulty and he tried to rationalize this unlawful mission with the money, but the amount of money was almost as insane as the project itself. Now as he walked, he understood that the money only intensified his guilt ... "whore," he thought.

Almost comically, he pictured the abstract in the Journal of Mammalogy:

"Abstract: Most previous studies involve the relationship of wildlife with its natural environment. This study was conducted to determine the survival of an extracted species in captivity for regularly timed blood removals to be sold to the Far East for ancient, medicinal purposes ... "

The guide stopped and they gathered around him, waiting for his words.

"Up there. See the marker above the snow?"

"How much snow?" Doc asked.

"Six, seven feet maybe." The guide sucked his lip nervously. "You sure this can be done without ... "

"Yeah. It can be done," Doc interrupted. "Whether we can do it is the question."

"You mean whether we get caught or not?" the guide said.

"No. I mean whether we die."

"That's what this is for," the guide replied touching his rifle.

"That is not big enough," Doc said flatly.

"It'll kill him," the guide whispered, "sooner or

later, maybe." They stared at each other before Doc turned and moved higher toward the marker.

"That's my point," they heard Doc say. "Later will kill us."

The ten-man team worked quickly, talking in hushed whispers at the marker. They unloaded their heavy packs, each man knew his job and, with cold-numbed hands, they erected a heavy tripod over the marker, positioning the block and tackle, tarps and medical supplies. Doc prepared the syringe on the jab-stick and two more backups. The guide stood behind them with the .458 ready, intently watching the steam hole, that connection between the outside and the darkened cavern of the bear, an umbilical cord between the mother and her powerful child. His hands sweated in the cold wind.

Suddenly, the crew was silent, all waiting, staring at the hole. Doc looked at them. "Anybody want to say a prayer or something?" They stared at him. He turned toward the steam hole.

"Forgive us, Father. I'm not sure we know what in the hell we're doing," he muttered. There was a brief pause and then, "Call the chopper. It'll be over, one way or the other by the time it gets here."

Cautiously the men enlarged the steam hole, their shovels easily penetrating the distance to the darkened ground. Beneath the snow, the entrance to the den was jammed with debris and Doc had to crawl into the snow tunnel to dislodge it, tossing rocks and earth behind him like a marmot. The crew watched from the outside as he worked for another thirty minutes, emerging and quickly disappearing again and again, clearing the entrance.

"I wouldn't do that for no amount of money," one whispered.

"He's crazy as hell … "

Doc's face appeared in the entrance, his headlamp on. "The jab-stick," he whispered.

Doc's assistant handed him the syringe and knelt beside him "You sure it's enough?"

Doc removed the needle cover. "From predening photos we calculated the weight at somewhere between thirteen and fourteen hundred pounds. I just hope it's not too much."

"Don't stick yourself," the assistant said, trying to smile.

"Yeah," Doc said and disappeared beneath the snow. He moved slowly down the tunnel extending the jab-stick in front of him, carefully protecting the large needle. The deeper he crawled,

the warmer the temperature became, the more
pungent the odor. No sound. Darkness, except
for the light reflecting off the snow — his heart
beat steadily, almost peacefully. He thought of
the big male's heart, beating only ten times per
minute with powerful pulses of rare blood.
Moving light. Black earth. Sweet smell. Spruce
limb. Stop.

The light moved revealing more soft-needled
limbs, grass … and hair. He stopped the movement of the light and then moved it ever so slowly, exploring more of the animal's tremendous
brown body. The light paused on the front paw,
ten inches wide with long, straight claws powered by a muscled shoulder that could break a
bull's back. The light moved up to the neck, gently caressing the long hair with its glow, moving
carefully with its dimness upward to the eyes.

The eyes stared at Doc lethargically, open and
sleepy, set in a tremendous head, drugged by
nature's winter needle. He lowered the light so
only the periphery of the beam caught the eyes,
the center of the illumination fell on the chest.
No movement. He watched for almost a full
minute before the massive chest enlarged and
fell. He extended the jab-stick, the needle quiv-
ered until the steel touched the long guard hairs

on the shoulder. Carefully guiding the needle through the hair, he touched the skin, paused, took a deep breath, and pushed firmly. The muscles spasmed around the needle and the giant mammal breathed quickly, out of sync. His eyes blinked and Doc tensed to exit quickly, but the muscles in its shoulder relaxed and the biologist slowly withdrew the needle.

Doc waited ten minutes without moving, watching the animal for signs of trouble with the drug. There was something wildly peaceful about the time, like watching an approaching thunderhead, powerful in its blackness. While pondering the creature before him, Doc relived the emotions of the past six months. He hated the people who devised this plot, on both sides. The need to trust the undercover contact with the Feds confused his sense of logic, but their threat of cutting off his grants, should he not cooperate, was even more alarming. The government seemed so impassioned about catching these corrupt people who dealt in drugs and illegal animal parts — almost as passionate as he about his research. And then there was the buyer, the strange, powerful man who craved the blood, who saw the future of this rare blood as if it were some new drug with potential for goodness, except there was no goodness … just money. Money. So he was trapped between the law and the perverse. Should he turn on one, his research was finished. Failing the other, he had been told they would kill him. He believed them. All Doc wanted, his entire life, was to be left alone.

He had carefully chosen his expertise so as to be removed from people and live in the remoteness of wilderness. He thought of the time it had taken to get his doctoral degree, all the demeaning jobs to pay for his education, the years he spent working for the research position at the university. He despised his place in this scheme, and felt a kinship with the creature beside him in this dark hole. He whispered. No one could hear. No one was present to call him crazy.

"I am sorry. They leave me no choice."

He paused.

"I would've understood if you killed me."

When Doc emerged from the tunnel his eyes were red and wet. The others noticed, but said nothing.

"Give me the ropes," he ordered.

"He out?" asked the assistant.

"Just give me the ropes," Doc snapped.

The guide moved closer with the big gun.

"Hey, Doc," he said and the biologist turned.

"Where's he going anyway?"

"I don't know. I don't want to know. Cage is a cage. I promise he won't like it. And I wouldn't want to be anywhere around him when he wakes up."

Doc looked out over the ruggedly beautiful land of Alaska's Kodiak Island. It stretched for miles below him, and, as the others watched, he disappeared with the ropes into the tunnel. At least he could find the creature, if need be, but the transmitter would be his secret. For what these people had done to him and the animal just below him, he hated with a passion unknown before in his life.

CHAPTER TWO

*A*t dawn Micah climbed the wooden steps of the fire tower overlooking a vast, timbered section of Hancock County, Tennessee. Upon reaching the highest platform she looked out over the graying landscape immediately noticing the absence of lights. No house lights. No car lights. No sign of humans whatsoever. The muscles in her legs felt oddly swollen, hardened from the climb and she lowered her pack as she sat on the steps that led higher into the locked observation room. She removed a dented Stanley thermos from the pack and poured her first cup, the steam rising straight up from the black coffee. No wind.

Moving to the rail, she watched as the land took form with the first light. With it came voices from scores of bird species claiming their space. She could recognize barred owls, whip-poorwills, cardinals, crows, and a thrush just below with its spiritual yodel and trill, her very favorite birdsong. A wild turkey gobbled prompting a chain reaction of gobbles around her, an avian overture of newness, a fresh start.

She pulled her cell phone from her pocket and dialed.

"Hello," the voice said sleepily.

"It's Micah," she said, "don't be mad."

"Have you lost your mind? Do you know what time it is?"

"I do," she answered. "I'm sorry, but I can only get the cell coverage from this fire tower and have a meeting in a few minutes ..."

"A meeting at daylight?" he questioned.

"With a game warden. They start early, but listen Bill, I'm going to need some more time."

"Listen Micah. You have to be in Alaska in thirty days. That project is finalized. The Melungeon angle is not priority. I just was following your hunch."

"It's going to be good, Bill. Trust me. I can feel it. How long have I worked for you?"

"Ten years Micah, and I've gone gray-haired since you started. You're a pain but a hell of a writer, and that's the only reason I put up with your theories."

"In ten years have I ever let you down?"

"No," he allowed reluctantly. "You've never missed a deadline ... yet."

"I'll make the Alaska date, Bill, but can you cover for me at the office, if I stay down here until then?" There was a long pause.

"Bill?"

"Yes. Yes. Okay, but get us something good. And I mean good, Micah. Different. I need something out of the ordinary. And another thing, don't ever call me this early again unless you're dying."

"Thanks Bill, I mean it. You're the greatest."

"Yeah ...yeah ...yeah ... be safe. Bye, Micah."

Micah breathed deeply looking down upon the land. With the growing sunlight she noticed an eerie hue, a green fuzziness of leafy growth. The earth looked old, its rounded knobs and darkened hollows seeming worn and mature, its forests providing homes for its children, both animal and human, season after season, year upon year.

She felt a great force of history here not unlike her first visit to Washington, D.C., but this energy was more primitive, more aligned to her soul, purer to the spirit, reflecting a kinship with the land that could not be explained to her satisfaction. The depth of it moved her like when she was a child staring innocently into a blackened, starlit sky, pondering eternity. The vastness of true wilderness touched her, its continuance without human interference embraced her, and its deadly innocence flirted with her in a wind-whisper along her neck. She shivered, then smiled, almost embarrassed with such pure thoughts of spiritual intimacy.

The shot was distant, the echo disguising its origin. Micah stared into the timbered ocean before her, wondering about the scene that took place beneath the greening forest canopy. The shot did not seem out of place. It did not necessarily mean murder or robbery, violence against man. It may only indicate food for tonight's table, no less acceptable than a fox taking a rabbit. The rules are different here, she thought. Backwoods rules. Wilderness rules.

*   *   *

The young officer tried to keep up, but Adam Shaw increased the distance between them as they ran. Although he was fifteen years senior, Adam's age was no detriment to his fluid movement in the woods. The rookie pushed harder, fearful of slowing the veteran's race to the shot, fearful of being judged less able by a man he immensely respected, and fearful of missing the action. Skirting the edge of the ridge they continued, jumping fallen timber, dodging dead limbs and skin-ripping greenbrier, never slowing in their pace whether uphill or down, leaping wet-weather streams and blowdown holes. The young officer had lost his hat a half-mile back and spider webs stuck to his face like hair strands of bubble gum. Quickly Adam Shaw stopped, kneeling beside a large oak overlooking a hollow below. The kid caught up, crouched with him and waited.

"They'll come down there. They'll be moving fast so don't wait too long to make the stop," Adam whispered.

"Okay," whispered the rookie.

"Fatboy'll stay put, but Luther'll run. Let him go and stay with Fatboy. Get his gun away from him. Quick. You understand?" asked Adam patiently.

"You're not even out of breath," the kid breathed.

"What?"

"Hell, I bet you're forty. What's your secret?" asked the young officer.

"Get his gun. Okay?" smiled Adam.

"Yeah ... get the fat boy's gun. *How did you do that?*"

Adam looked at him. "You tracked them at a dead run for a mile," the kid said. "There was no sign. I may be a rookie, but I've been in the woods my whole life. I'm good and there wasn't any sign."

"I'll be around. See ya, kid." And Adam was gone, disappearing into the undergrowth like a deer. The kid leaned his head against the oak and tried to catch his breath.

Reaching the next ridge, Adam Shaw became motionless again, studying the dogwood as he waited, lightly touching the crimson-tinged petals of the flower reflecting the crucifixion blood, following the trunk crooked and small so as to never be used for such a thing again. A crow called behind him, a perturbed, irritated caw. A blue jay joined in. It was then that he heard them running in the leaves below. The two poachers passed within twenty yards of the wildlife officer, Luther carrying the dead turkey flopping lifelessly over his shoulder.

Farther down the hollow the rookie's heart was pounding. He heard them coming fast, just like Adam said. They ran into his view a hundred yards away, Luther in the lead with the flopping bird and Fatboy with the gun. Behind them moving silently was the form of Adam Shaw. A ghost whose presence was questionable, he dissolved into the leaves and trees, a movement of blurred reality. Cooper's Hawkeye in the flesh, the kid smiled to himself, and he stepped calmly from his hide into plain view.

Luther never broke stride. Upon seeing the uniformed officer, he flared like a decoy-wise mallard, circling away from the kid and gaining speed.

"State wildlife officer! Stop!" the younger officer yelled and Luther gained even more speed. Fatboy, on the other hand, stopped dead in his tracks, breathing hard, cradling the twelve gauge in the crook of his massive arm, staring with squinting eyes at the approaching lawman.

"Howdy," the kid smiled.

Fatboy stared some more.

"Fine lookin' ol' piece ya got there. Mind if I take a look at it?" the officer said.

Fatboy spat a stream of tobacco juice that dribbled across his whiskered chin. "Ain't ya gonna chase 'im? He's a gittin' away."

"Lemme have the gun. We'll talk," the young officer tried.

"You ain't gittin' my damn gun."

The kid smiled. "You as out of breath and dog tired as I am?" he asked.

"Hell, yes. Luther's like a damn coonhound. Run my ass ragged," Fatboy said.

"Hey, I know what you mean. I'll tell ya, friend, that ol' gun makes me nervous as a cat. How 'bout restin' it against that dogwood there so'ns you and me can talk peaceful-like and rest our tired bones?"

Fatboy thought as he worked his chew. He eyeballed the kid and then casually leaned the shotgun against the tree. "You're new at this, ain't chee?"

The rookie sat on a section of soft, green moss. "Green as a gourd," he said. "Hell, have a seat. Let's me and you get acquainted while we wait for your partner."

Fatboy struggled to sit on a fallen log, his shirt bulging at the buttons, exposing tremendous layers of belly fat beneath the flannel.

"Partner, my ass. He ain't no partner of mine. What county you work, anyway?"

"Just hired on in Grainger," the rookie said.

"This ain't Grainger. Hell, yore lost as a goose."

"I'm in training," the kid smiled.

"Who's yore trainer, Casper the ghost?"

"No, well, sort of," he reversed. "The Finder. He's workin' me."

"The Finder. He's here?" Fatboy asked.

"Yep. Chasin' Luther."

Fatboy threw his head back and horselaughed. "Why didn't youins say the Finder was here?"

"I just did."

Fatboy laughed again, shaking his head, the belly fat like some grotesque moving white fungus on the log.

Adam watched as Luther tossed the bird and settled into his run on the ridge, but no matter what evasive action Luther took, the following footsteps remained. Adam enjoyed watching Luther run in front of him, but was concerned about Fatboy and the gun and the rookie he left behind. He had run Luther five miles before, but had no time for such a marathon now.

"Luther!" the Finder yelled.

"What!" Came the reply as it moved.

"Where are you goin'?"

"Finder! That you back there?"

"Yeah!"

Luther stopped running, resting against a large white oak. Adam caught up quickly, stopping at the tree. "I didn't know it was you, Finder.

Where'd you come from?"

"Behind you," Adam said.

"Oh."

"Let's get the bird," Adam instructed.

"Who's the piss ant?" Luther asked.

"New man. Named Henley," said Adam softly.

"Oh. Well, I'm caught. Let's get on with it. I got to be at work in a hour."

"Fatboy ain't drunk, is he? I left him with the kid."

"I reckon I run most of it out of 'im," Luther smiled showing his missing front teeth.

"I appreciate that," said the Finder.

Luther breathed hard for a few seconds before offering, "By the way, just a heads up. Story goin' round is that Billy Browder is out to getcha. Really pissed about you arresting his pappy."

"Maybe," the Finder said, "he'll see fault in staying mad. I find no future in it, myself."

*　　　　*　　　　*

Smitty saw the Toyota parked at the fire tower and pulled in behind it. Opening the door and stepping outside, he overturned his spit-cup, spilling the brown goop on the floor of the truck.

"Hello!" came a call from somewhere above. Smitty looked up to see a figure high in the tower looking down.

"Come up!" she yelled. "The view is spectacular!"

"I've seen the view, Ma'am! Why don't you come down?" Smitty watched as she moved down the steps and then he grabbed an old shirt from behind the seat and mopped the mess from his floormat and quickly tossed it into the back of the truck. He wiped his hand on his uniform pants as she extended her hand.

"Hi. I'm Micah Rogers."

"Name's Smitty, Ma'am. Nice to meet you."

Micah smiled. "So, Smitty, do you hate me?"

"No ma'am. I just don't reckon I can help you."

"You're Shaw's supervisor, aren't you?"

"Yessim."

"Then you can help me," she said.

"How'd such a young woman get so many 'tics?"

"Tics?"

"Politics, ma'am."

"Maybe I'm not so young," she offered.

"I get a call last night from my Regional Manager who'd got a call from the Director who'd got called by National Geographic in Washington. Everybody pushin' me to get you hooked up with my man, Adam Shaw."

He paused. She just smiled.

"You try talkin' to Adam about this story you're doin' before you pulled the politics?" he asked.

"Sure did. He says he's not interested."

Smitty leaned against the truck and rubbed his head "And why not, you reckon? No offense intended, ma'am."

"He says it would infringe upon their privacy and he could think of no honorable reason to do that."

"And what do you say about that?" Smitty asked.

She smiled at him. "I say these people are an amazing story — their history, the mystery of their roots. I say that nobody's history is private."

"This ain't got nothin' to do with wildlife, ma'am."

She thought and smiled again, taking a position next to him on the truck. "Wildlife Officer Shaw is the only non-Melungeon that they trust. Wildlife Officer Shaw is under your supervision. Wildlife will suffer if relations are strained between all of us who value our natural resources."

Smitty laughed. "That's a threat. I believe you just threatened me."

Micah laughed. "Is it?"

Smitty's laugh fell. "Melungeons are people. They have nothing to do with Adam Shaw's job, unless they violate the law and then he'd arrest them, which ain't got nothing to do with you. Any trust between Adam Shaw and these people is personal and I have no jurisdiction over that. You can call my boss and his boss and the President of these here United States, but that don't mean nothin' to me, or Adam Shaw. You see, little lady, all those people you're callin' ain't here. Look around. You see any of 'em around here anywhere? Just me and you. You gotta deal with me, and I ain't dealin.'"

"Then what'd you come for?" she asked.

"He asked me to. The Finder asked me to," Smitty said.

"The Finder?"

"That's what he's called, Adam, I mean," he said.

"What's he find?" she asked.

"Anybody that's lost, ma'am."

She looked at him. "I don't think he wants to talk to me."

"Yes, he does. Tonight," he offered.

Micah looked at him. "I thought … "

"He said you had good hands. He asked me to study them."

"My hands," she laughed, suddenly not knowing what to do with them.

"Yeah."

"And … "

"And I don't know nothin' about a woman's hands. Imagine that," Smitty said spurring an uncomfortable pause, a break in the tension of their words.

"Tell me something about him," she said. "How long have you known him?"

"Ten years, I guess. Showed up for a job interview and I liked him. Never regretted the decision to hire him on."

"Where's he from? Where'd he go to school?" she pried.

"Like he said, I reckon a person's history is private."

She smiled.

"Well, listen, I gotta go," the old game warden smiled.

"Yeah. Me too," she lied.

"Don't forget," he said.

"Where does he live?"

"Newman's Ridge. See if you can find him." And Smitty started the truck and was gone, leaving Micah to stand there studying hands and intentions and game wardens that were unlike any law enforcement she had ever dealt with in the past.

*   *   *

They walked two miles back to the truck after issuing Luther and Fatboy citations for hunting turkey in a closed area. The kid carried the feathered evidence, switching the dead weight from one hand to the other, one shoulder to the other.

"That's the largest human being I've ever seen in my life," the kid said.

"Right healthy specimen," Adam said, moving the old 12-gauge to the crook of his arm. "You smile like I told you?"

"Yessir. It was either smile or cry, and I didn't figure crying was real good for our image."

"Treat him with respect?" Adam asked.

"Hell, Finder, we damn near had a picnic while you chased Luther."

"It's useless, you know — a common problem among game wardens. Had a major problem with it myself a long time back," stated Adam flatly.

"What's that?" the kid asked.

"Cussin.'"

They walked a while without talking and then Adam stopped. "If Fatboy had pulled down on you with the twelve gauge, would you have killed him?" Adam asked seriously.

"That's what they've trained me to do," Henley said.

"That's not what I'm asking."

Henley paused. "I don't know, Finder. I truly don't know."

"You might want to study it. So at least if you have to make the decision sometime, it'll be made with proper study and forethought," Adam said.

The kid watched as the Finder walked away and then hurried to catch up.

CHAPTER THREE

O ne hundred miles to the southeast, Zeke Thompson and his three child-hikers had turned away from the Nolichucky River in Unicoi County at noon. The trail was gentle, the first mile following the river before turning into the trees. He watched them closely at first, checking on stamina and attitudes, careful to mentally record those data requested by his major professor. It was the strangest assignment of his graduate program, foreign to his regimented methods of scientific analysis, vague and in his opinion, subjective.

A hike along the Appalachian Trail with three

very gifted children would be followed by psychological testing to determine the effect of wilderness on creative energies, a phase of environmental values yet to be documented or evaluated. The federal grant, allocated jointly to the Departments of Psychology and Natural Resources respectively, would revolutionize the thrust of environmental sociology, he had been told. "Why me?" he remembered asking.

The department head looked over his glasses and the pile of papers on his desk. "Here's what they want," he had said. "A doctoral candidate with extensive knowledge of the Appalachian wilderness, including wildlife, medical training and a personality that would make the kids comfortable." He looked up from the paper. "Is that you or what?"

"I'm no baby-sitter," Zeke complained.

"These aren't babies," the professor said. "You've got one here ..." He fumbled through the file. "Peter something. Genius pianist at seven. Writing his own concertos. Played with the Boston Pops. He's twelve. And this Conrad kid, he's fourteen. His paintings go for more than you'll make the first year out of here. And Anna. Now here's one for you. Total recall. Had the Bible memorized at ten — with comprehension. Taught a special studies course at Vanderbilt in theology last year. She's also fourteen."

"And you want to put them on the A.T.?" He asked. "Do you have any idea how that might affect them?"

"What do you mean?"

Zeke smiled in amazement. "You guys kill me. The whole world revolves around your grant listings."

"That's survival, Zeke."

"Why not get some wildlife guy?" Zeke asked.

"You find me one with a psychology background. Nonexistent, but don't change the subject. What do you mean, about the effect on them?"

"Fear. Pure, raw intimidation. Y'all have been watching too much Disney."

"That's your job, Zeke. Make it pleasant for them. Take all their fears away. Let them experience the grandeur of the mountains."

Zeke rose from his chair and moved to the door.

"Hey." Zeke stopped.

"Three days. Two nights. Your future could depend on it," the older man stated.

Zeke turned, not smiling. "Please don't threaten me, sir."

"Then don't let me down, Zeke. This is important. Think about it. What if we can eventually document that nature, unmolested nature, changes the mind's capabilities to create good things. Not just art or music, mind you, but economics, urban planning, politics — everything. You should be flattered we chose you."

Zeke paused. "I want parental authorizations and liability releases. Personally, you understand. Not for the department," said Zeke flatly.

"What's the paranoia?"

"Paranoia? Three child prodigies, overprotected their entire lives," Zeke said. "Mix that with your total ignorance of the grandeur of the mountains and I feel suddenly very alone."

"But you are doing it, aren't you, Zeke? You do understand the politics of survival. You are part of us, aren't you, son?"

"I'm not your son. Not by a long shot. And you know what? You should take a long walk in unmolested nature. It might improve your negotiating skills, with all due respect, sir."

A blue jay screamed, bringing him back to the trail and the three little people in front of him. Jared led the trio. The painter. The oldest. He walked with an intriguing loneliness, his eyes scanning the trees around him as if searching for a lost friend, removed from the others through his concentration. Zeke could not tell if he was happy or sad, content or afraid. Second in line was Peter, following the larger boy, torn between a would-be bond with Jared and the safety of the man behind him. Out of place. Misplaced. Trying to be brave in the eyes of Anna, the girl, who followed him. Anna who captured them all with her mere presence. The female child, whose smile overwhelmed them all, whose words floated like feminine chimes upon their ears.

"I have a question," she whispered as she walked. The boys in front immediately stopped and turned. Zeke leaned upon his staff, smiling as they formed a loose semicircle around her. "We aren't talking. We walk and walk and look and feel, but we don't talk. Is this some sort of male thing, 'cause if it is, okay, but it's really hard on girls … "

They looked at her.

" … I mean we like to talk. A lot." Her eyes met theirs hoping for a smile, a nod, a signal of understanding.

Zeke waited for one of the boys to answer, but the silence continued. "I've got no problem with talking," he finally said. "Let's talk."

"It's like an intrusion," Jared whispered.

"He speaks!" Anna yelled. "Look, did you guys see it? Lips moved and everything!" Jared turned, hiding his smile, but the others caught it and Peter laughed.

"Okay," Anna continued. "This is good. We're

---

getting somewhere now." She put her hand on Jared's shoulder and grabbed Peter with the other. "Jared speaks and Peter laughs. We're friends now, even though we just met. Can you guys feel it? We are friends. Right?"

"Right," Peter laughed.

"Right?" she jerked Jared's shoulder.

"Sure," Jared smiled.

"Good, now I have an important subject to discuss," Anna said. "I've been praying and praying as we walked on how to bring this up without being embarrassed. We are together for the next three days. My bladder cannot stand three days without some relief, SO, how do I take care of this problem tactfully?"

"I'll go along with whatever God suggested," Jared said.

They all laughed. "It's really not as bad as you think. For example, you see that big tree over there?" Zeke pointed.

"Yes."

"It's big enough."

"Okay," she laughed. "Now, here's the game plan. You guys have to sing or something until I get back."

"Sing?" Peter asked.

Anna moved off in the direction of the tree, urging them with her arms to take up their voices.

"What did you mean, intrusion?" Zeke asked Jared. They focused on the man now and his question.

"I feel like an intruder," the young painter said.

"Why?" Zeke asked.

"I don't know. Do you?" the boy returned.

"Yes," the guide said.

"Sing!" Came a yell from somewhere behind the big tree.

CHAPTER FOUR

$\mathcal{T}$he worm moved, powering its destiny deeper into the center of its universe, thinking not, only existing in the burning energy of being. Unaware of its host or the pain its life caused, it moved and ate, relentlessly working toward an unthought goal of continuance.

The bear groaned at the wriggling movement deep within its brain and then in a frenzied madness of frustration attacked a nearby rotting log, biting and slashing and roaring, woodchips flying with sod and moss and leaves. It bit at the air with a popping of jaws fighting a maddening unseen enemy.

Quickly it stopped, its head weaving on quivering vertebrae, staring up into a canopy of unfamiliar leaves, held tight to limbs it had never before seen, trunks of trees that looked vague, out of place in the wildness it remembered. It sat like a huge dog, drugged by the sudden peace of stillness within its brain. Shutting its small eyelids, a lightened darkness came and with it, visions of its brief captivity.

Darkened cavern with hard, rounded, straight limbs it could not chew through. The sickening scent of the two-legged that brought food. Little white suns that burned its eyes. The ring-tail that chattered above, just out of reach. Sleep. A burning urge to fight, but no power to move. The songs of strange fliers somewhere outside its cave and a lost sense of day and night. Rage. Anger. Fear. Power. Limbs that suddenly gave way and screams from the two-legged. The crunching, gurgling bone-breaking cries. Limpness. Sticky-thick red wet. Running into the light. More cries. Light. Air. Trees. Pops. A burning along its shoulder.

The creature took the burning blows from the distant pops and moved toward the trees seeking refuge in that land containing no smelly two-leggeds, away from the compound that had been its cage, and those who had taken its blood and raped its instinct for solitude. Once inside the timberline it roared again, the voice of a thousand years of ancestors who, likewise, sought the safety of wilderness, the womb of the land.

The feeling of crunching leaves under its feet was not comfortable and as far as it could see was the forest floor and there was a hot, wetness in the air that made its breathing more labored, but it continued up the slope of the mountain. Soon the animal was cooler and the shaded green of the rhododendrons soothed its spirit. Its instinct was to hide in the thicket of smooth green leaves and tangled limbs, but another spirit moved it on, up again through the hardwoods of the next ridge and across, through the tangles of laurel and rotting logs and flowers unknown to its memory.

Birds cried as they followed above, marking its path, for its presence was menacing to those animals that saw, or heard, or smelled it, creating a strange presence of magnificent fear and instinctive death. The bear's track was northward, innocently carrying with it a maddening insanity that made the mammoth carnivore fight demons in the air and devils in rotting logs, and sit dog-like in the Appalachian sun trying desperately to still its palsy-trembling head as it swayed back and forth, back and forth, with tight shut eyes.

CHAPTER FIVE

*M*icah was lost. She had traveled the back-woods roads of Newman's Ridge for an hour, following directions sparingly given by three locals who looked at her like she was the center attraction in a freak show. In the dusky light she crept along in the Toyota, looking for some sign of recognition.

She saw a man beside the road working in the ground. Rolling the passenger window down, she saw he was digging what appeared to be a small grave. The truck engine idled smoothly.

"Excuse me, sir?" Squinted eyes stared at her from under wrinkled lids that jerked nervously. "Can you help me find the game warden's house?" she asked.

"I'm busy. Can't leave." A nervous twitch rustled his whiskered cheek.

"No, I mean can you give me directions?"

He tapped the shovel handle with an amputated finger. "Sure, anybody can."

She smiled, hiding her frustration. "Would you please tell me how to get there?"

"From here?" he asked, tapping the stub faster, with the remnants of a fingernail clicking against the wood.

She turned off the Toyota, got out and walked around the hood to the man in overalls on the side of the road. Her eyes caught a short arm with fat, infant fingers lying stiffly beside the fresh mound of earth. Plastic. A doll dressed neatly in frilly white prepared for a morbid burial. She looked back at him. "Yes, from here," she said.

"You wanna fight?" he asked, grabbing the shovel handle.

"No. I need directions."

"You jumped out like you wanna fight. I'll smack yore damn head, woman."

She stared at him. "Where does Adam Shaw live or do you even know?"

A yellow jacket buzzed his lips. He caught it in the air, squeezing its juices between his dirty, yellow-calloused fingers. "Stilly Holla. Anybody knows that."

"Where's Stilly Hollow?"

"That way," he pointed in front of the truck and she noticed the still pumping abdomen of the yellow jacket hanging by its stinger from his hand.

*　　　　　*　　　　　*

It was almost dark when she found his house, entirely by accident. The forest-green state truck was parked under a massive oak in the front yard some two hundred yards off the main road. The house was of log construction with a large covered porch extending on two sides. Micah engaged the clutch, letting the truck idle forward down the long graveled driveway. Remembering his voice on the phone, she tried to put a face with it. She had developed a game of sorts, matching voices with future faces. They never turned out the way she pictured. Adam Shaw's voice had a deep, rolling coolness with an unseen smile attached to it. An eternal optimist, she smiled. He's probably fat and has acne, she thought.

The light from inside the house spilled out onto the porch as the door opened and his silhouette filled the door space. Leaning against the doorjamb, he watched her approach from the truck and she, studying his outline, immediately tossed out the fat theory. A mottled, brown dog stepped forward onto the porch and growled. She stopped. A whippoorwill started up behind the house. She watched the man watch her. The dog growled again with more intensity. They stared at each other across the yard, the dog's lips quivering between them.

"What's his name?" she finally asked.

"History," came his voice across the grass.

"History," she said to the dog. "Come." The dog looked quizzically at the man in the door.

"It's okay," he said to the dog. The cur moved quickly off the porch to Micah with a sudden change in personality and she knelt to greet him. Adam walked to the steps and sat.

"Where'd you get the name," she asked between dog licks.

"He came with it. Friend of mine took the pup home as a present to his new wife. They named him, History, 'cause she said if he messed on the floor, he was history."

"I take it he messed up," she said.

"Sometimes a fella can improve his status in life through his mistakes," he said smiling.

"A philosopher, too."

"Added to what?" he questioned.

She wrestled with the dog, lessening the apparent importance of the conversation. She was thankful for History's presence, a tool she could use to cover the unexplainable giddiness in her stomach. The absurdness of it frightened her, made her angry both at herself and Adam Shaw for his ability to affect her. "Surely there's more," she returned.

He smiled at her, directly at her this time and she could partially see his blue eyes through the half-light of dusk, contrasting with his closely cropped dark beard, not unlike the way his deeply tanned forearms contrasted with the faded denim shirt. "Just like there is more to old June Bug Barnes," he said.

"Who's that?"

"You met him earlier. He had a shovel in his hands, I believe."

"How did you know about ...?"

"He called me. He isn't crazy, you know."

"The man was burying a doll," she said. "Where I come from, that's not normal."

"He lost his daughter fifteen years ago," he said. "She just disappeared. And his wife was found the following year frozen on the mountain. They say she was obsessed with finding the girl and was never quite right afterwards. So June Bug buries a doll every so often to have the funeral that never happened. There must be a hundred doll gravesites around these parts. He says he hopes to get one close to where his daughter actually died. And you are right. You are not from here."

She pushed the dog away and the cur quick-stepped to the man on the porch. Micah changed positions and sat cross-legged in the grass. She looked for his eyes, but the light was gone now and she wanted desperately to see his face. "There are no preliminaries with you, are there Mr. Shaw? No nice casual exchanges between two people who know nothing of each other."

"Does that bother you?" he asked.

"I'm not used to it."

"Is that true?" he asked.

"Pardon me?"

"Nice, casual exchanges. Preliminaries. You really want them?"

She paused. "I said I wasn't used to it," she said truthfully. "Sometimes it gives you time."

"I see," he said.

He stood and moved to the door, his boots making solid contact with the wooden boards of the porch. "Would you like some ice tea or I think there's some lemonade," he asked while pausing at the door.

She waited before answering. "How 'bout something stronger. It's been that kind of day," she said.

"Muscadine wine's about the best I can do. It's pretty good."

"Anything's fine," she said.

The sky was black now and the stars focused white dots above her. She pondered whether to move to the porch or remain in the clovered grass. It was soft beneath her hands and the yard retained a fragrance of honeysuckle and mint holding her there.

The door squeaked and she saw his outline move through it carrying a jug and a glass. He paused on the porch, looking in her direction. She wondered whether he was contemplating moving to the grass with her or whether he felt more comfortable on the porch. She waited, strangely hoping he would step off the porch, but he turned and placed the jug on a wooden table. Quickly, Micah stood and moved to the porch. Nearing him at the table, she smelled his presence close to her, a mixture of clean jeans and soap-scrubbed skin. She heard the liquid move from the jug into a glass as he spoke.

"Ever had muscadine wine?" he asked.

"No. Is it strong … I mean powerful?"

"If you drink too much," he said.

"How much is that?"

"Depends on the drinker, I'd say," he whispered.

She saw the form of his hand reaching toward her and she met it and she spoke. "He scared me," she said softly.

"Who?"

"The man with the doll," she said.

"See, now you're relaxed," he said. "There's no pretentiousness in 'He scared me.'"

She tasted the wine, the smell of it interrupting the yard smells. "That's good!"

"You like it?" he asked from the porch rail.

"Yes. So you think I'm pretentious," she answered.

"Over the phone, yeah, you were, like some business lady on a mission and the only thing in your way is a bunch of backwoods idiots to be overcome with nice, casual preliminaries."

She took a seat in a wooden rocker facing him. It squeaked as she moved, wood against wood. "You've never seen my hands. How come you told Smitty I had nice hands?" she asked before sipping.

"Miss Louise at the post office told me. She watched you address an envelope."

Micah laughed. "Is there anything I've done here that people haven't told you?"

"Please don't misunderstand," he said. "They are not just calling me. Everyone is calling everyone about you. You're the talk of the town. The only reason they call me is because you're looking for me."

"Well, what will they say about me here tonight?"

He laughed at that and she noticed his laughter was caught by the trees around the yard and seemed to hang mysteriously in the leaves before disappearing into the darkness. "It's just the way they are," he said.

"You know what bothers me?" she whispered.

"What's that?"

"I can't see your face."

He paused. "I can't see your hands," he added.

"I'm sorry," she said.

"Why?" he asked.

"I've been judgmental. You're right," she said. The whippoorwill changed positions in the yard closer to them and began a furious calling. "But I'm very good at what I do," she continued.

"What is it you do good?" he asked.

"I write about cultures. I can portray them truthfully."

"Most writers are afraid of the truth. They're not brave enough."

"I'm brave," she said. "Give me some more of that stuff."

"So, what do you know about Melungeons?"

"Lots," she said as she sipped. "A dark-haired people of unknown origins. Found in the mountains in the late sixteen hundreds. The women are supposed to be beautiful. Because of extreme persecution, they withdrew into the deepest parts of the mountains. Some say they are of Portuguese decent; others, the lost tribe of Roanoke. Some believe the twelfth tribe of Israel. What do you think?"

"Tribe of Israel?" he questioned.

"Yes."

"That's a new one," he said.

"Not really," she said. "You ever heard of the Bat Creek Stone? Found down around Loudon."

"No," he said.

"It was excavated from a mound in 1889 by a field assistant with the Smithsonian and on this stone was a series of inscriptions that were thought by some to be Paleo-Hebrew from the period of 100 B.C., hence the theory that we had pre-Columbian visits by Old World cultures. If claims of the Bat Creek Stone's origin are true, that might mean that there were Old Testament people right here in these mountains."

"I don't know anything about where they may have come from, but I know that they are a very closed society," he said. "Extreme persecution forced them to be. They have no written record of their past, no stories for their children to hand down. Their bonds are in their historical mystery. They believe, I think, that they have a purpose. They even have their own language that is hard to understand. And you want to talk to them? Why would they talk to you? Even if you could understand them — which you can't — you can't even talk to the common mountain folk."

"Yes, I can."

"You ever been tattooed?" he asked.

She paused. "You mean do I have a rose on some secret part of my body?"

He laughed. "No. Tattoo has a different meaning up here." He paused. "You can't talk to them. All you know is what you've read. That's dangerous."

"I'm talking with you," she said.

"Yeah, but I'm easy."

She could feel him smiling in the darkness of the unlighted porch. "Right," she laughed. "I haven't apologized to anyone in ten years and you had me backing up in three minutes."

They paused again, the night sounds becoming louder with their silence. "So, educate me," she said. "What does tattoo mean in mountain talk?"

"It's a practical joke using twine and nail and the cabin wall. They play the string setting up some wild vibrations and sounds inside the cabin. Makes you think the haints are inside."

"Haints?"

"Yeah, like spooks or spirits," he explained.

"I don't believe in spooks," she said.

"What about spirits?"

"I believe in spirits," she said. "Like muscadine wine."

"Are you hungry?" he asked.

"No," she said. "I want to stay out here in the dark drinking homemade muscadine wine and never seeing your face."

He smiled, though she only felt it again in the darkness.

"This is great, you know?" she said.

"What?"

"Saying exactly what I'm thinking to a total stranger," she replied.

"Why is it great?" he asked.

"Being brave is exciting, don't you think, Finder?" He didn't answer quickly. She waited for his words to float across the porch and with the delay she sensed for the first time, his struggling for words.

"That's a hard one," he whispered. "I reckon I'd rather say what I feel and be comfortable with the words than feel excitement because of them."

She sipped the wine and thought, his words confusing her with their simplicity. "You're not comfortable with excitement?" she whispered back to him.

"It can be dangerous."

"That's bad?" she asked. "But your whole life is dangerous. You face death every day."

He changed positions on the porch rail, leaning his back against a column. "My death would not be dangerous. Becoming lost is where the danger lies."

"Lost from what?" she said.

"The truth," he said plainly.

She stared at him across the darkness. The sky flashed to the east behind the outline of his face. "I told you I'm brave," she said. "The truth doesn't scare me."

"Is that so?" he asked.

"Yep. So, what'd ya say? Be brave, trust me, Adam."

"Them are eyebrow raisin' words."

"Really?" she said.

"Yep, around here you ought to pay attention to someone who says, 'Gee, I never really thought about sellin' that dog,' or 'trust me.'"

"I guess it boils down to instincts then," she said.

"Or faith, maybe," he added.

"Trust me," she said leaning closer, "and I'll buy your old dog."

"Be brave," he said, "and I'll give him to you."

Micah laughed again, never once contemplating the color of his eyes.

CHAPTER SIX

*T*he bear had moved steadily north, occasionally stopping to cool itself in the security of rhododendron thickets along the way. Hunger now overwhelmed it. Unfamiliar with the life forms, it had tried a variety of food items, including a tuber dug with its massive paws that sent legions of screaming, stinging needles to the inside of its mouth, a pain so intense that it became confused with the haunting madness of the wriggling brain worm, creating an ironic pleasure in pain, a horrid, unnatural desire to cause injury.

The bear smelled them first, a pungent, moving odor of musk. Remaining motionless in the thicket, it slowly turned its head, focusing on the tunnel trail and the sounds of moving animals. A wild boar stopped abruptly in the trail upon seeing the massive form blocking its path. The sow grunted, standing stiff-legged, with its piglets gathering around.

The bear charged in a blurred roar of mountainous power, crushing the vegetation like a howling, pelted tornado, paralyzing the hog's instinct to flee in a leg-trembling preamble to the screaming attack. Staring submissively at the approaching death, the hog felt a stunning blow to its back and passed into nothingness. The hog's progeny squealed in the undergrowth, running in random directions, hearing the bone-crunching behind them. It fed on the kill immediately, consuming the life form before the hog's eyes dimmed.

*   *   *

Doc had been drunk for three days when the phone rang in his trailer. The ringing triggered a deep throbbing in his brain and he fumbled for the receiver to stop it.

"Hello," he mumbled.

"Are you alone?"

"Who is this?" Doc asked.

"It's me. Remember my voice?"

Doc paused.

"Yes. What do you want, now? I thought I was through with you."

"We have a problem. The bear has escaped. I may need your services again to help get him back."

Doc sobered quickly, pressing the phone against his ear. "You fools."

"Can you find him if we can get you in the general area?" the voice said.

"Maybe. Where is he?" Doc asked.

"Somewhere in Appalachia ... maybe the Smokies."

Doc closed his eyes trying to make the pain go away.

"We'll pay you well."

"Keep your damn money," Doc said.

CHAPTER SEVEN

*T*hey had reached Curly Maple Gap four miles into the hike, after ascending steadily through Jones Branch past rhododendron and tremendous hemlocks, some stands of which Zeke had told them were virgin. They made camp at Curly Maple Gap an hour before dark. The shelter had been constructed of concrete, probably in the forties Zeke had said, and it provided protection on three sides, but was open in the front. After supper, they laid out their sleeping bags and stored all their gear, separating the food and suspending it between two trees some distance from the lean-to. The fire popped in front of them, its living golden light reflecting on the inside walls of the shelter. Zeke moved to the other side of the fire and sat on a log looking back at them across the flames, the darkness of the mountains looming large behind him.

"Why so quiet?" he asked. A chestnut limb popped in the fire sending a shower of blue amber sparks skyward. They followed the rising little lights with their eyes in front of him.

"It's very dark," said Peter.

"Is it the darkness that makes you quiet?" Zeke followed.

"Yes," said Jared. "Because it makes you think more."

"Thinkin' instead of talkin'," Zeke clarified.

"Yes," the boy said.

"About what?" Zeke asked.

"Lots."

"I feel so small," Anna interrupted.

"In a bad way small?" Zeke continued.

"No. It's a wonderful sort of small," she smiled.

"I find no wonder in feeling small," said Peter.

"I keep thinking about all the people before us that lived like this, every day, all the time," Jared whispered.

"A note is small, Peter," she said.

"A note?" Jared said.

"Yeah, a note in a big symphony."

"I admire them," Jared whispered again, his vision locked into a glowing coal.

"Who?" Zeke asked.

"The pioneers. You can see it on TV, but it's not the same out here. It's hard," Jared answered.

"It's darker, too," Peter said.

"It's bigger," she said.

"What if a bear comes?" asked Peter.

Zeke poked the fire with a stick causing the wood to shift and settle, sparking the blackness above them again. "Then we might get to see a bear," he said smiling.

"You have a gun?" asked Peter.

"Why would you ask that?" Zeke asked.

"You have a gun?" asked Peter again.

"I was raised in these mountains. I have a gun. We won't need it though."

"Then why do you have it?" Jared asked.

"I promised my father a long time ago," Zeke said. "It would be the same as your parents saying, 'Wear your seatbelt.' Anyway, black bear are timid. If one came it would be after we're asleep and we'd never know."

An owl called behind them, laughing and crying and another answered close by with the same eerie sounds and the night was suddenly alive with sounds they had never heard in such a big darkness so far from beds and lights and towns.

"What's that?" Peter said with big eyes.

"Barred owls," Zeke said. "They're having a fine time, huh?"

"Yeah. I guess," Peter said.

Zeke paused and tilted his head back and then reproduced perfectly the owl call. He oohed and aahed and barked and suddenly they heard wing beats in the darkened air above them like primitive heartbeats of moving air from some living nighttime being that occupied the mountain of darkness around them. The owl settled in a tree above the fire fluffing his feathers and popping his beak and they watched the light reflective in the large rounded eyes staring down at their circle of eyes. The bird voiced with a low, guttural note that seemed unlikely to have come from such a small creature. Yet it seemed insanely logical in the spirit of flighted mountain night feathers that hunted with sharpened talons and an innocent taste for blood. The owl looked again and flew, gone from their vision before the air finished moving beneath its wings.

"Why'd he come?" Peter asked.

"My call invaded his airspace," Zeke said.

"Reminds me of a poem," Jared said.

"Which one?" Anna asked.

"I can't remember. I'll think of it," Jared said.

"Tomorrow we'll do twelve miles. Make sure you take good care of your feet. Let me know if blisters start and we'll take care of them," Zeke said smiling.

"I'm suddenly sleepy," Jared said.

"Me, too," Peter agreed.

"How 'bout you, Anna?" Zeke asked.

"Not really. It's too nice to sleep," she said.

"It's fine sleepin' out here," he said.

"What about you?" she asked.

"I'll stay with the fire until you guys are snorin'," he offered.

He looked at them across the flames, their young faces flickering with reflected yellow light, and wondered about their thoughts, if they were that diffcrent from when he was a kid. He thought about the darkness, about himself, the barrier between its terror and its gentleness, for without his confidence, his understanding of the wilderness night, owls become flying demons and gentle bears become maddened nightmares.

They talked for another hour until Peter simply lay in his bag and was asleep. Jared lasted another twenty minutes before becoming a non-participant in the talks and when they looked he had fallen asleep, head in hands, elbows resting on his knees.

"I've seen you before," Anna said.

Zeke looked puzzled. "Where?"

"In a dream," she said.

"I doubt if it was me," he said.

"I think it was," she said nodding her head. "I was afraid, but you were there to help me."

Zeke smiled across the dying fire. "Well, I'm glad I could help out, even in a dream."

"Well, you know how dreams are," she said. "You can feel the truth of a dream without the faces."

"Tell me," Zeke said. "I'm curious how someone your age could give lectures at universities on spiritual matters. It's all very confusing to me. There is so much disagreement over doctrines and interpretations of scripture."

She smiled. "The faith of a child is strong," she said. "I don't listen much to the arguing over doctrines." Anna pointed to his chest. "Listen from within you. We have been given a gift to understand the truth, but it's within us, and it is a personal truth between the Father and each of us."

Zeke watched her face in the fire's light. "I

have always felt closer to some greater strength out here. How has wilderness affected you on this trip? I have talked to the others. I mean I can understand how wilderness influences painters and musicians, but your life is different."

"True wilderness separates us from the arguments of man," she said smiling. "It allows one-on-one time with the Father."

"And you are how old?" he said.

"Old enough to know that I am not strong enough without His help," she said.

Zeke smiled. "American males are taught that we're supposed to be strong. Handle everything. You know … John Wayne stuff."

"We're talking two ideas of reality here. One lasts. One does not," she said. "I'm going to pray before I sleep. Will you pray with me?" she asked.

Zeke paused. "That's kind of personal, Anna, praying I mean."

Her smile fell, as if slapped away by some invisible hand and Zeke saw it.

" … what I mean is that I'm not used to praying with anyone. Maybe you could and I'll listen along," he tried.

She stood in the firelight and moved slowly around its glowing coals toward him. Taking his hand she knelt beside him and bowed her head.

He watched her, waiting for her words, but she never spoke, and he glanced back at Jared to see if he was watching and the boy was sleeping and when his eyes returned to the girl her eyes remained closed for a long time, so long in fact that his hand went to sleep in hers and it tingled and twitched as she prayed silently. Finally she stood and released him.

"I didn't get to listen, Anna."

She smiled. "In words?" she asked.

"Yes," he said.

"Words," she whispered. "So primitive, but I prayed for both of us, in case you weren't listening."

"Thanks," he said looking up at her.

And she disappeared behind the fire into her sleeping bag, leaving him alone with the fire and the darkness of the mountain behind him.

CHAPTER EIGHT

*M*icah opened her eyes. She saw the curtains move slightly in the open window
and then they were still again. Pulling the ter-
rycloth bedspread closer around her neck and
turning to face the window, she welcomed the
soft warmth of the Downtown Motel's bed. It
embraced her, wrapped around her. The furniture was not motel furniture, more southern
Appalachian; the motel was no kin to a Holiday
Inn, but rather a converted department store of
the fifties, remodeled to provide home-like
rooms for those few travelers who found need to
stay briefly in the hills of Hancock County.

The phone rang on the antique bedstand, its call attacking the stillness of the open window. She fumbled for it.

"Hello," she whispered hoarsely.

"You up?" his voice asked.

She looked at the clock beside the phone. "It's six o'clock."

"Yes, it is," he said.

"No."

"No what?"

"No, I'm not up," she whispered.

"I see."

She felt the weight of the phone against her left ear as she closed her eyes, feeling comfortable with the pause.

"Are you still there?" she mumbled.

"Pick you up in twenty minutes."

"I'm sleepy," she whispered into the phone. She closed her eyes again and waited for his reply.

"Somebody died," he said.

She opened her eyes. "Who?"

"An old man I know."

"I don't understand. What old man?" she asked.

The curtains moved. A dog barked somewhere on the street, a crow called above the window.

"You ever heard of a sin eater?" he asked.

The bedspread fell from her shoulders as she suddenly sat up, revealing a Washington Redskin football jersey.

"A what?"

"A sin eater," he said.

"No."

"Twenty minutes," he said again.

"Okay," she said.

She brushed her teeth in the shower to save time, the water finally getting good and hot as she stepped out. She toweled quickly leaving the small of her back wet — sticking to the clean shirt as she tucked it into her jeans. Fresh socks never slide over wet toes, she thought, cramming her socked feet into the L.L. Bean boots, waiting to tie the laces after brushing her hair and sloshing a shot of Scope. She stopped briefly to examine herself in the mirror.

"Where am I going?" she asked herself, leaving the mirror in a blur, rummaging through the closet and emerging stuffing a pair of slacks and shoes into a leather backpack, along with her 35mm and three rolls of film. She was out the door in nineteen minutes, contemplating her flapping bootlaces as she ran down the hall.

He sat waiting in front of the Downtown Motel, the idling engine offering the only man-noise to the morning. Their eyes met and she smiled, moving quickly toward him and jumping in. As the door slammed he smelled her, a clean, soap-flower scent that filled the space around them and then was gone. He pulled away from the curb as she placed the pack between them and began tying her bootlaces, her thick hair falling forward. She stopped suddenly as he found fourth gear leaving town.

"You're dressed up," she said tossing her hair behind her shoulders with a quick twist of her head.

"It's just a tie."

"Where are we going?" she asked.

"A funeral service, of sorts."

"Why didn't you tell me?" she asked and pulled the slacks and shoes from her pack.

"You're fine the way you are," he said.

"It's no trouble. Changing is not a problem," she said.

His fingers found the knot and pulled, the tie slipping from beneath his collar. He handed it to her.

"It doesn't matter," he said.

She folded the tie and placed it on the seat.

"Was he a friend?" she asked.

"I knew him. Mostly I know his family."

"Why are you taking me?"

"You wanted to meet them," he said.

"Melungeons?" she asked.

"They'll stare at you. You will consider it rude. They'll stare," he said.

The truck bounced over a wooden bridge and he turned onto an obscure gravel road, going through the gears again.

"Why are you doing this?" she asked.

He looked at her. "You asked me to trust you. I do. No cameras. No recorders. Stay close to me and watch. Don't stare back at them. Be respectful of their grief. Don't speak unless you whisper to me."

"What if they speak to me?"

"They won't," he said.

"Will it cause you a problem that I'm there?"

He swerved to avoid a fallen limb in the road. "Yes."

She watched him drive, his eyes, his hands on the wheel in the sun's light for the first time.

"Thanks," she said.

"You did say you were brave, right?" he said.

The truck hit a mudhole, splashing the windshield.

"What's a sin eater?" she asked.

"Are you brave?" he asked again.

She looked at him. "You know I am."

"I know you're persistent."

"That's not what I mean," she said.

"What do you mean?"

She smiled at him. "I want your ol' dog."

There were old cars and trucks parked randomly around the house that was tucked between old oaks at the head of the hollow. A rare spring fog lay suspended above the ground and thickened in height obscuring the treetops and surrounding ridges. It fell wet against the windshield as he killed the engine and she felt a green, watery cold surround them.

She walked close to him as they approached the porch with dark eyes from twenty heads watching them, staring, just as he had warned. She wanted to take his arm as they walked, and the feeling grew stronger with each step until she could no longer stand the brushing of their arms and took his arm, first with her left arm and then with her right hand. She took refuge in his arm, and was thankful that he did not pull away in the fog on this mountain under the gaze of these strangers that penetrated her confidence.

They moved onto the porch among the dark eyes and the silence continued. She looked straight ahead, through their stares, noticing that the door was a painted an old powder sky-blue as was the porch ceiling. She smelled strong tobacco and a wet dog and hickory smoke and she saw flashes of baggy kneed trousers and faded jean overalls and a blackened fingernail and scarred boots and an angry skin cancer on the back of a freckled hand, but no eyes because she would not meet their stares. Finally, the Finder's arm moved, pulling her through the blue door into a large room inside the old house. It was like in a funeral parlor and they could find no empty chairs so they stood in a vacant spot against the wall as every eye turned to assess them.

She stood on tiptoes and whispered into his ear. "Why didn't they speak to you?"

He mouthed the word without sound as she watched. "Punishment."

"For bringing me?" she mouthed back.

He nodded without looking at her. She looked down between her feet at the wooden floor and then back up into the room to meet their stares, but they were not looking anymore. The room had drawn their attention — and the body lying in front of them in the dim light.

Micah stared across the room, over the bowed dark-haired heads, some moving with sobbing grief, others stilled with a silent, throbbing emotion that filled the empty space within the walls of the room, thick like a ghost fog, hanging web-like between them, touching their spirits with a mountain presence of death, imprisoned by the walls and ceiling of that old house and its funeral room, a place of past deaths and spirits and tears.

Somewhere behind them a door opened and the men from the front porch filed into the room and gathered around them against the wall, pushing closer so that she could smell them and their mountain lives in the air around her. Another door opened behind the body and a man moved through the dim light in front of the grieving family. He held a black Bible in his right hand and he began to pray, chasing the ghost fog from the room with the fire and brimstone of Appalachia soul, the black book swinging in the air amongst words of Holy scripture, a song and chanting of distant words that merged like some native fire dance of musical spirits, until he collapsed against the wall in a wide-eyed sweat, leaving the sobs and cries of the family alone in the room with the slowly returning ghost fog of death.

The crying stopped when the old woman entered the room. She hobbled through the mourners on short fat legs, carrying a tray covered with a red towel. Resting the corner of the tray on the coffin, she removed the towel and laid it across her shoulder, exposing a small plate and glass, which she placed upon the dead man's chest. The woman retreated, waddling back through the door behind her.

Micah stared, wishing desperately that she could photograph the scene before her, trying to freeze it in her memory. She wanted to record all the smaller parts that made the whole: the smooth grain of the pine box and the dead man's whitened hands clasped above the edge, the glass of dark liquid and the plate with some breaded food, the sunken cheeks of the man's bearded face, with a large nose above coin-weighted lids that she couldn't see.

The Sin Eater entered the room from the porch and the mourners parted, heads bowed, as he passed before them. They did not stare at him, she noticed, and she intently watched the Sin Eater and those who would not look at him. For the first time she had complete freedom to observe the room and feel its life force without fear of intimidation.

The Sin Eater lacked the fire of the preacher; he came with a gentle movement through the people, almost humble in his step. There was a sunburn line across his forehead, leaving

whitened skin extending into his receding hair-
line that she thought almost like a halo born
from some sunny hayfield baptism. He moved to
the coffin and stopped, the back of his white
shirt centered in the dim light. He stood there a
long time, head bowed, arms extended to the
body and then he ate from the plate and drank
from the glass, removing the coins from the dead
man's eyes when finished.

Micah raised herself to whisper, but Adam
squeezed her hand with his arm and she quickly
lowered her head. The Sin Eater turned to face
the people, the women on his left and the men
on his right and from their ranks stood one man
and one woman and both began praying with
different words so that she could understand
neither of them, a conglomeration of mountain
prayers, segregated by gender and joined by the
room itself into one human cry before it ended.
The Sin Eater whispered amen and they all heard
him and he walked through them toward the
door and they reached across their spaces to
touch him as he passed — out of the blue painted door and was gone.

She caught Micah's eyes and smiled — a small
girl about ten with long black hair and gray eyes.
She moved from the front of the room toward

Micah, weaving around the mourners' legs and over chairs until close, never losing the smile or the beauty in her eyes. They all watched her as if the ceremony had lost its importance and the movement of the girl toward Micah overtook it. Micah released the Finder's arm and lowered herself to the girl's eye level and smiled.

"I was afeared you wouldn't come," the little girl said.

"I'm sorry?" Micah started.

"Lord God!" came a cry from the room as the girl extended her hand to take Micah's, leading her from the room by the path already cleared by the Sin Eater, through the blue door and into the light of the sun.

CHAPTER NINE

*T*he water ran clear, gurgling over and around the smooth rocks, pooling and stretching around them as Micah and Adam sat perched on two separate boulders saying nothing.

Finally he looked and saw her eyes staring at the water around her bare feet.

"You okay?" he asked.

She looked up at him across the water between them, one boulder to another. "I don't know," she said. "I don't understand."

"The child," he started, and then his eyes left her and his words were lost in the sound of moving water.

"Finish it," she said. But he didn't. She looked into the water again and spoke. "In the old days there were angels who came and took men by the hand and steered 'em away from danger. There ain't no white-winged angels these days."

He looked at her.

"That's what she told me, the first words out of her mouth when we were alone in the yard," she said.

"What's it mean?"

"You don't know it?"

"No," he said.

"*Silas Marner,*" she answered.

"Who's he?"

"*He's* a book," she said smiling.

"Maybe the little girl liked the book," he offered.

"No," she said. "She's never read the book."

"Are you sure?"

"I'm sure of nothing," she whispered.

"Well," he said.

"It's my favorite book," she said looking at him.

"You made it fine through the blue door," he said.

"What?"

"The blue door. Haints can't enter under the blue of the sky," he said.

"I ain't no haint," she said.

"I know."

She continued. "But men are led away from threatening destruction; a hand is put into theirs, which leads them forth gently towards a calm and bright land, so that they look no more backward; and the hand may be a little child's."

They looked at each other. "That's the end of it," she said. "The next part of the paragraph she didn't say." They remained silent for a while watching the moving water.

"The child," he said, "is special. A blessed child. She has never spoken before today. That's what amazed them."

"Never?"

"Not the first word," he said.

"How is she special?"

"She will replace the Sin Eater when he dies. The first female to hold such a sacred position," he explained.

"Why, Adam? Why was she chosen?"

"Story is that she sees the future and draws pictures." They were silent for a long time.

"Where's the calm and bright land, Adam?" she said finally.

"Beats me," he said. "I've been lookin' my whole life."

*   *   *

They drove the back roads in silence, each alone with private thoughts. Micah seemed lost in the land, only aware of her own presence inside this natural place and her position alongside him. Watching him drive, her head resting on the window glass, she pondered ideas foreign to her, in regions of thought exploration never before visited. She wondered what it was that prompted these thoughts, whether it was he or the land or the people. She knew not, but the thoughts scared her a bit, for she strongly believed that her thoughts produced fruits of reality and she had no inkling as to the fruit growing inside her. No color. No taste. No hint of the tree that bore it. Just a feeling of depth, reaching far inside her, that made her stomach queasy from its power.

He looked at her across the seat and their eyes held until he looked back at the road. They crossed a bridge, the smell of the water below invading the truck.

"Why would they have a service that early in the morning?" she asked.

"They call the Sin Eater pretty quick after death," he said. "Whenever he can get there is when the service starts. They don't embalm, you understand."

"Do you believe in sin eating?"

"Do you believe in baptism?" he responded.

"I asked you."

"I believe it gives them comfort to have chosen one clean of spirit who can symbolically remove the sins of the dead. It connects them to the spirit."

"Do you believe it?" she asked again.

"It makes no difference what I say I believe, unless … "

"It does to me," she said.

"Why?"

"I don't know. Maybe there's an answer there. Maybe it would make me feel better," she said.

"You're probably just hungry. Let's stop up here and eat," he said.

She saw the store in the distance, an old building with a concrete front porch and chairs. Antique drink signs hung on its sides, not displayed as antiques, just never taken down. Several old cars were parked on the side and there was a truck getting gas from a Sinclair pump in front.

They pulled in beside the other cars and got out, then made their way toward the steps on the front porch. The man came from somewhere behind the camper at the gas pump. Adam had just enough time to glance in his direction before the short piece of two by four hit the wildlife officer behind the ear and the attacker was upon him, swinging and yelling, Adam's blood painting the white gravel beneath him.

"NO!" Micah yelled, and quickly she was on the man's back, choking and pulling until he slung her sideways against the porch. She saw him closely for the first time as he neared her, younger than she first thought, but the madness in his face made him appear older.

"I'll kill you too, bitch," he slurred.

From somewhere on the porch a dark form passed before her and the assailant was overwhelmed by a tremendous man who didn't need a stick because his fists were like hammers, pounding away at the struggling form below him. She glanced behind her at the men huddled on the porch of the store, looking down at the spectacle before them, who watched the Finder slowly get up and approach the violence, kneeling at the head of the fallen attacker, grabbing the flailing arms of his rescuer.

"Stop! Fatboy!" he yelled. "No more!"

Fatboy looked into the Finder's face before grabbing the bloody hair of the man below him.

He raised the man's head, looking squarely in his eyes. "You cowardly sombitch. You and yore Daddy both ain't worth sweat off the Finder's ass. I'd kill ya right here, ifn the man didn't ask you spared." Fatboy got up and waddled back to where Micah still crouched against the porch. He helped her up. "You got grit, lady," he said and then disappeared onto the porch.

The Finder lifted Billy Browder up and leaned him against the nearest car. He looked at Billy's face, the cut running deep under his right eye where all of Fatboy's weight powered the first punch. "Hey, Jeter, get me some wet towels," he yelled to the porch.

"Leave me be," Billy mumbled.

"You need stitches," Adam said.

"Leave me be!"

"It's over, Billy. Let's move on."

"I wish I'd killed ya," Billy said.

"Not really," the Finder said. "You'd like it if we were okay, but you can't figure out how and take up for your daddy at the same time. Nobody wants to hate nobody, Billy."

"I like it," Billy said. He tried to smile but his lip was busted so it didn't look like one.

The Finder took a towel and washed his attacker's face, Billy jerking his head away at first, but then slowly allowing the towel to take away the blood. Everyone watched from the porch, including Micah. They listened intently trying to hear the words that passed between the two men, amazed at the scene, amazed at the Finder. "It'll drive you crazy, trying to make sense of hate. Real confusing. Tell you what, I'll buy you a beer. I'll buy your ol' man a beer. We'll talk about it. But know this Billy Browder, I consider you a friend. I'll not speak badly of you."

He left Billy at the car and climbed the porch steps, stopping at the top, looking down at Micah who stared up at him.

"C'mon, let's eat."

"I'm not hungry," she said.

"Hey, Billy. You hungry? C'mon, let's eat a bite," Adam offered.

Billy looked at the Finder. He tried to smile again, but it hurt so he just shook his head.

"You're one crazy son of a bitch," he said.

"Think so? C'mon, she won't eat with me. I'll have to eat alone with Fatboy if you say no."

"You keep him off me?"

"C'mon," the Finder said.

Billy moved toward the steps, his head bowed. Adam looked at Micah again and winked. "C'mon," he said again. "I thought you were brave."

"Who are you?" she said.

"I'm your lunch date," he grinned.

"You need a doctor. Your head is cut real bad," she said.

She took a towel and made him sit, cleaning the wound. Billy passed by and entered the store as if nothing had happened. "Talk to me," she continued.

"His father was the judge in the adjoining county. I arrested him for killin' deer out of season."

"You arrested a judge?"

"Yeah. Caught him good. Then my judge sent him to jail. Said he wanted to show that no one was above the law. Then Billy's dad cussed my judge in open court and got more time for contempt. Had to spend time in jail and when he got out, his own county fathers fired him."

"I didn't think you could fire an elected official," she said.

"You can't legally, but they did. It stuck — said he was an embarrassment to the good folks of their county."

"What about Billy?"

"He just loves his father. Can't fault a man for that," he said.

"He tried to kill you Adam."

"But he didn't."

"What if he tried to kill me?" she asked.

"That's something else," he said.

She knelt in front of him. "Well, why didn't you just forgive the father for the deer thing, you're so big on forgiveness?"

"I can't forgive sins against man's law," he replied. "Sins against me are another thing."

"So, if he had killed you, splattered your brains on the ground, that's okay?" she asked.

"Who could have stopped him? The second I saw him I was hit. I'm not much on brooding about what I can't change. You ever had pickled pig's feet?"

"What?" she asked amazed.

"Harold's got the best around. C'mon, let's eat." He looked at her again. "The future, Micah — never the present. Control of my thoughts in the next five minutes ... there's my chance. The future is built five minutes at a time. Then my past has a chance to become meaningful."

He took her hand and escorted her through the door into the store where all of them gathered and ate, the recollection of the incident floating above them for a while before disappearing all together, except for Micah, where the whole experience settled in her thoughts. She wanted to take him home and care for his wounds and ask him a hundred questions that seemed to escape her at the present, untangling the mystery of his strength, so that she might know, beyond any question, that he was real and she was connected to him.

*   *   *

In the afternoon, after the storm had passed heading east into the mountains, she watched him sleep on the couch in his den. She had driven him home from the doctor's office, after the eighteen stitches, and the pig's feet and Fatboy hugging her goodbye and Billy Browder apologizing to her on the front steps of the store. It seemed all out of sync to her, the memories hopscotching in front of each other until there was nothing left but her vision of him asleep on the couch. She watched him for a long time, lost in the feeling just being there, at that particular moment in time, with this man, in this house, in this country, with these people. After a while she retrieved her journal from the pack and wrote:

April 30 *This day is the strangest of my life. How could I have lived all these years and been so comfortable with my position, to be so confused* *now? I wish I could watch CNN to see if something monumental happened today, like the earth shifting its axis or something, distorting the reality as I knew it and we must play by different rules now. But he owns no TV and I wouldn't, no I couldn't leave here. I would be afraid to leave. I am not afraid here. That's the weird part of it. It's not a confusion that scares me, but draws me deeper into it, like falling asleep and wanting to never wake because it's so peaceful in this new place. The confusion is in the past, I think, and he said I should not dwell there, no he said he should not dwell there. I should live for the next five minutes, just like he said. I must find the young girl again. I must find her. She is the answer. I must find her.*

She moved from the desk to the back porch and rested her arms on the rail. The sky was clear above her, but to the east, above the mountains, the storm flashed with quickened lightning that lit up a black sky and left her feeling safe somehow, alone on this porch with the Finder sleeping so close to her.

Gary Cook

CHAPTER TEN

*T*hey had emerged from the woods at Indian Grave Gap like misplaced wanderers, thrown back to a time when the land's spirit and man's were always mingled, two spirit forces becoming one, mixing like a violent drop of blood in moving, healing water.

Zeke was surprised. The children had adapted well, no longer moving like beginners, complaining not, questioning often. He noticed an extraordinary quality that had emerged in the three — perhaps begun by Jared but quickly embraced by Peter and Anna — of speaking in whispers on the trail as though normal voices would offend the land and represent a sign of dis-respect. Zeke quietly loved them for their sense of intrusion. He wondered if it had something to do with their genius, their enlightened percep-tions that might give them the intuition to feel reverence for the land's spirit. He wondered that as he walked behind them, quietly directing them through the mountains.

From the top of Beauty Spot they observed the Black Mountains to the south, Roan Mountain to the east, Big Bald and Flattop Mountains to the southwest, and the Toe River Valley. They also could see the Nolichucky River, their beginning point.

"We've come that far?" Peter asked.

"Yeah," Zeke said.

"On foot," he smiled. "That's cool."

"Why?" asked Zeke.

"Why what?"

"Why is that cool?" Zeke repeated.

"I feel free, maybe for the first time," Peter said.

"From what?"

"From the land beyond where we started," Jared added.

"Then where are we headed?" Zeke asked. They thought about that.

"The center of the womb," Anna said finally,

looking down at her dusty boots. "The beginning."

They all looked at her, even Zeke. She looked up at them and smiled and they all just stood there for a long time.

Before dark they made it to Cherry Gap and set up camp. The concrete lean-to was sufficiently large to accommodate all their bags and gear. The wind smelled of rain, the wet, cold freshness that precedes dark clouds. Anna stood in the trail and looked west toward the black line of clouds moving toward her. They flashed with light and she heard the thunder almost a full minute later, a low rumbling proclamation of power from above. She felt a lonely, sinking feeling in the pit of her stomach, like the restless feeling of fall or a memory long lost of something that was meaningful, but not completely recalled.

The wind came two hours after dark, at first wafting the fire sparks around in little circles and then coming in full-blown gusts that bent the trees. Thunder shook the ground and they sat inside the concrete shelter looking out into the violent blackness as the rain came, tremendous drops at first, then smaller ones, but with more velocity. The noise was so loud that they had to yell to be heard.

"Will it blow the shelter over?" asked Peter.

"It's been here since 1962!" yelled Zeke. "Don't worry!"

Lightning struck a tree fifty yards in front of them and the trunk exploded, the light and sound stunning their senses. Anna grabbed Zeke's arm and screamed. Peter wanted to, but didn't. Jared stared ahead and smiled, his heart beating wildly at the power of it. The air was suddenly electric and their hair stood out. Lightning struck again and again around them and the light from their lantern illuminated their forms, making them appear almost comic, like clowns from a wilderness circus, hair without gravity and flashing smiles of teeth and thunder-mixed laughter. A ball of light floated in the darkness, the size of a grapefruit. It moved toward them and Peter scrambled for his camera yelling "Oh please ... oh please."

"What is it?" Anna asked.

"Ball lightning," whispered Peter. "It's never been documented but everybody knows it exists. There!"

"Can I touch it?" whispered Jared.

"No! You hear me! Nobody move!" he yelled as he brought the camera to his eye and they all watched with awe as the ball of light floated between them.

It moved like a dancer, so smooth and delicate and intense, its direction guided by some natural law unique to itself. They could hear the shutter from Peter's camera and him whispering "Oh thank you, God!" but they could not take their eyes away. They followed the ball as it floated among them, around their heads, as they dodged its path. Blue sparks began to concentrate around them as the ball began to fade and they pointed at each other, the blue auras taking human form under the roof of the shelter in the rain and thunder and night.

Zeke saw it first, the blue shape of something horrible in the darkness in front of the shelter. He paused, as if in disbelief, but the thing was clearly visible, its blue-haloed head weaving back and forth upon a massive body, black eyes staring into them while St. Elmo's fire danced wildly off its form, an electrical creature of fur and power and death.

Zeke struggled with the vision before him, knowing it real and knowing it impossible, confusing his ability to trust either reality. The creature rose to its full height, sniffing the air and stepped forward toward them. Zeke's hand slid toward his backpack and found the zippered compartment. His hand sought the handle of the pistol. It seemed so small now, so terribly small and insignificant. Never taking his eyes from the animal, he spoke, trying to be calm, but failing.

"When I move, roll over face down. Put your hands behind your neck. Don't move. Play dead. Understand?"

"I ... I ... I ... thought you said black bears wouldn't hurt us," whispered Peter.

"It's not a black bear ..." Zeke whispered, almost to himself.

The creature fell to all fours, splashing into a pool of water sending a shower of spray toward the light. Zeke moved toward it, waving his arms and yelling. The boys rolled to their bellies and hid their eyes, but Anna watched, moving toward the shelter opening, knowing from her dream that Zeke would protect her and the evil would die, for her dreams never lied and her Father in Heaven was present.

Nothing prepared her for what she was about to witness. The charge was horrific, the power of it unstoppable. She heard a gunshot, and saw Zeke fall to the ground rolling into a ball as the devil-creature seized Zeke's head in its mouth, shaking the man as if he was weightless, as a dog would shake a rat. She heard the snarls that over-powered the thunder and Zeke's scream that ended abruptly when his neck snapped and he was flung sideways into the darkness, leaving the creature in the center of the light still alive and terrible. Anna stepped sideways into the darkness, her mouth agape with horror and shock and sickness from the bile rising in her throat.

The bear rose again in the darkness, trying the air for another scent of the female that maddened it, moving closer to the lighted shelter and the two-leggeds that remained there. Peter could hear its footsteps close to him and he could smell the creature and hear its quickened breaths just above him. Suddenly, the creature roared, its foul breath rolling over the child and Peter began to cry, wetting himself in his terror. He felt a tooth crunch into his skull and another just below his eyebrow. Unable to hear his own screams, a mysterious calm seemed to come over him, he felt the ripping of his skin yet somehow remained detached from the pain until there was blackness and brief memories of his mother's face and the smell of her neck.

Anna heard the boy's screams and they seemed attached to some great fear of dying and helplessness and pain and she turned to run into the darkness from whence the creature had emerged, running away from darkness into darkness to escape, falling often, scraping her face and arms against the hard branches of nature's web.

Jared dared not move, not breathe. He played a game of mind control, picturing the most beautiful scene of his short life, a small girl on the beach, playing at the edge of the surf as the sun went down behind her over a smooth sea. He could hear the waves and smell the water and he was happy with this thought so he tried to paint it in his mind, choosing colors from his palate, feeling the brush in his hands. It blocked Peter's screams and the sound of the creature ravaging Anna's pack, and he did not see the bear plunge its nose into Anna's clothes filling its brain with her smell, moving away into the night, its nose to the ground like some prehistoric hell-hound trailing the girl's footsteps over the rain-washed mountain.

*   *   *

He was forty-six, the hiker who came across the scene the next morning. He had done the Appalachian Trail six times since 1969 when he had returned from the war an outcast, having endured the terror and confusion of needed values to stay alive, a confusion that left him questioning the value of life if it required that to stay alive, but the power of the trail had soothed him, the aloneness of it befriended him — until now.

He saw the young man sitting by the dead fire, using a piece of charcoal to sketch some scene on the back of a clean, white T-shirt, the bodies of Peter and Zeke lying in plain view, sprawled unnaturally, staring sleepy-eyed at the sun that had seen nothing of the horror the night before. He knelt beside the young man who sketched a scene of a young girl on a beach, and recognized the faraway look of shock. "What happened here, son?"

Jared looked up and smiled. "I told them we were intruding," he said.

"Who did this?"

"It was a bear. It was a big bear. It was a grizzly, I think," Jared said.

"There are no grizzlies here, son."

Jared looked at the man for the first time. And quickly he was crying. "Then what was it ... what was it?" he moaned.

And the hiker held the young man, there on the trail in the center of the womb and they cried for a long time between the bodies of hateless death, unable to change the violence in their heads, only fraternal in their pain, this young painter of beautiful things and the old soldier of bloody jungles. Their only strength was in their compassion, a yearning for return to goodness.

GARY COOK

CHAPTER ELEVEN

*J*ared slept after the interview and the sheriff
stayed in the room for a long time watching
the boy's eyes jerk behind closed lids. Finally, the
lawman stood, moved to the door and quietly
closed it behind him. The smell of the hospital, a
sour-clean scent, was stronger in the hall where
he stood leaning against the wall. Someone
moved through his peripheral vision and spoke.
" … bear attack."

"What?"

"Sheriff, you okay?" The sheriff just looked at
him.

"I understand the boy reported a bear attack."

"Who're you?" demanded the sheriff.

"Brent Harris. Special Agent with the D.E.A. Is there someplace we can talk?"

"Let's move outside. I can't tolerate the smell of this place," the sheriff said.

The birds were singing outside and the air was sweet. They left the sidewalk and moved to the shade of a large white oak where the sheriff leaned against the rough bark and noticed squirrel cuttings beneath his boots. "We have kind of a situation," Harris said.

"No shit. I'd be callin' two dead, one little girl missing, a real situation."

"It could get worse," Harris said. "Did the boy describe the bear?"

"Yeah, determined it to be big and blue."

"Blue?"

"Blue," repeated the sheriff.

Harris paused. "Where are the bodies?"

"The funeral home."

"Have you seen them?" asked Harris.

"The older feller is broke all to hell, but at least he's in one piece. The kid, well. He ain't so lucky."

"Can I see them?" Harris asked.

"Wait just a damn second," demanded the sheriff. "You best be explaining what the D.E.A.'s got to do with this bear?"

Harris looked down at the ground, then back up. "I just came from Georgia, a place way back in the mountains where a similar attack took place. There was a cage built in a barn that housed a bear. We traced the owner of the farm back to a man we've been after for a long time. Does a lot of business in China ... drugs and animal parts."

"What's the bottom end of the stick?" asked the sheriff.

"There's a grizzly loose on the Appalachian Trail, Sheriff."

"A grizzly bear. Waal sir, is the beast blue?"

"No, but he's real big. An adult grizzly. Over a thousand pounds," said Harris.

"Truthful?"

"Yessir."

"Some circus bear, I reckon?"

"He's made two hundred miles in six days, tracking due north. I can assure you, he's no circus bear," Harris stated.

"What are you a tellin' me? A wild grizzly bear is in these here mountains?"

"I don't know what the hell to tell you," Harris replied, "except we have to get the Appalachian Trail closed to the public and find that bear."

"What about the girl?" asked the sheriff.

"Do you really think she's alive, Sheriff?" the government man asked, knowing the answer.

"No, I don't."

"No, I don't either. Who's up there now?"

"Rescue squad ..." the sheriff paused. "Maybe thirty men."

"Are they armed?" asked Harris.

"They ain't got no grizzly bear guns, ifn that's what you mean."

"Get them off that mountain, Sheriff," Harris demanded, "right now! Clear that mountain and close the trail."

"The hell you say?"

"I have a man coming. He's a bear expert. He can find it and bring it out. I need you to help us out."

"You can kiss my ass, Special Agent Harris. I'll be needing some more information before I join your game. Sounds peculiar to me."

Harris looked away, then quickly back. "You ever had an operation go bad, Sheriff? Something happen you never expected?"

"Keep talkin.""

"We'd been after this guy for five years and finally got a man in, somebody he trusted. This bad guy wanted a bear, a grizzly bear, as a source of drugs for the China market. You know, the Chinese think bear blood can make them super studs or something. The covert team got him the bear. They made the arrangements. They were just ready to bring the whole thing down — five years of work — and the bear escaped. Now the bear has killed innocent people. We need to find that bear so others don't die. The team made a big mistake. The bear should've never been moved, but it was and I'm here to try and resolve this thing and end it. We can make it worth your time to help us. You need a campaign fund? I can provide it. You need better equipment? Just name it. *Whatever you need, just say the word.* Just get that mountain cleared of people so we can get that bear back!"

"I've called a press conference this afternoon," the sheriff said.

"Cancel it," Harris said seriously. "I'll handle the press."

"Waal, since you're so keen on handlin' the press yourself, I guess you wanta take care of the kids' folks too."

"No thanks."

"I figured," spit the sheriff.

"What about the girl's parents?" Harris asked.

"Her folks were missionaries. Kilt when she was three, somewheres in Africa. Her grandpa's a comin."

"Hell of a thing," Harris said. "We gotta deal, Sheriff?"

"I don't know."

"You don't know," Harris looked hard at the man.

"That's right. Things could go wrong," replied the sheriff.

"Like what. All I'm asking is to clear the mountain and keep your mouth shut."

The sheriff paused, looked at the ground and then back up quickly. "Okay," he said, "but you hear me good. Keep that son-of-a-bitchin' game warden from Hancock County away from here. He'll ruin it all. Hell, I bet people have all ready called him and *he'll find that girl and the bear too.* The son of the devil, he is."

Harris looked puzzled, "Who?"

The sheriff smiled. "Like you boys don't know him. You jest mind what I say."

"*I don't know him,*" the agent protested. "What the hell are you talking about?"

The sheriff paused again. "He's the problem. That's what I'm talking about. He can find anybody … anywhere. It ain't natural how that man can find lost people."

"Well he's *your* problem," Harris snapped, "and if you can't handle a local game warden, maybe I got the wrong man to help me."

The sheriff smiled. "You done waded a little deep

in the river to be worryin' about that, wouldn't you say, Agent Harris?"

"Can you handle it?" Harris said flatly.

"Yeah, I can handle it, Agent Harris, and I will get you a list of my needs," he said. "Just curious, what you gonna tell the press?"

"We're working on it."

The sheriff spat. "You're workin' on it. Should that make me feel better?" he asked.

Harris paused. "No," he said.

CHAPTER TWELVE

S he stood on the porch for a long time waiting. Finally, Micah entered the house
through the unlocked front door and step by
step searched the unlighted rooms for his presence. At the end of the hall, in a small room
lighted by one small lamp she found him. He sat
with his boots resting on the window sill, his eyes
transfixed by the view outside the open window.

"Hi," she whispered. A breeze moved the curtains and his eyes found hers. "What's wrong?
Something's wrong," she said.

"I have to go," he answered to the room. "I'm
not sure how to do this. It's strange."

Micah moved closer. She smiled. It was a different smile, a different face that held eyes of compassion he was not accustomed to. "Hey," she said. "Talk to me."

"Why are you here?" he asked. "Tell me."

Her smile fell. "I'm not sure anymore. I knew at first. Not now," she said.

A mockingbird called outside the window and then it was quiet again. "There's been a bear attack in the mountains and a girl is missing. I'm going to find her."

"A lost girl?"

"Yes."

"Black bear attacks are rare, aren't they?" she asked.

"Very rare in these parts," he answered.

"Can I go with you?" she asked.

"No," he said.

"Why?"

"If you go, I may not be able to find her."

"What difference could I make?" she asked.

He paused. "I do better alone," he said.

"Adam. What are you talking about?"

He paused again. "We don't know each other," he said.

"That's not true."

"Yes, it is."

"What? What do you want to know?" she asked. She waited for an answer.

"You don't understand," he finally whispered.

"That's right. I don't. I don't understand any of this. But I don't care."

He looked at her. "You could die if you go."

"I want to go," she said.

"Why?"

"What do you want me to say?" she said opening her arms.

"The truth," he said.

Micah paused struggling for words, reluctant to lie, yet terrified that she might become vulnerable to a truth that she did not understand. She stared at the floor and then into his eyes and then outside, through the window at a blue sky. "I could tell you that it's my job," she said. "It would be a great story, but that is not completely true. I'm afraid that if I lie, even a little bit, you will know, and . . ."

She looked at him and continued. "I've never known anyone like you, so I don't know how to find the truth. You have somehow become the truth to me and I feel strangely alone when I'm not with you."

"I am not the truth," he said quickly.

She shook her head in frustration. "See ... you

give me nothing, Adam. There's no hint of your real feelings toward me. You're patient and kind. You're like a guiding hand leading me somewhere I've never been. Is that an attraction, or the way you are with all women?"

"What women? I don't have anything but real feelings."

"Tell me the truth about how you feel about me and I'll know how to answer your questions," she said. She took his hand into hers, staring into his face.

Adam Shaw leaned forward. "You said you were brave, remember?" he said. "Then be brave. Brave enough to understand that *I don't know* what part you will play in my life."

"But you do know already," she whispered. "I can feel it and you won't tell me."

"I can't tell you things I can't describe."

"You can try," she pleaded.

"Think of the girl, Micah. Her name is Anna. She's fourteen and alone in the woods. She saw some terrible things. She's scared. Be my friend, Micah. Think of the girl."

"What about me?" Micah asked. "Maybe I'm scared."

"Whenever I get scared, I think about somebody else. That's what I'm doing," he said.

"You're scared?" she asked.

"Terrified," he whispered.

She just sat there, looking at him. "Of what?"

He said nothing.

"Okay," she sighed. "How do you know she's not already dead?"

"She could be alive. That's all I need to know."

"What did the girl see? Anna, what did she she?"

"Things no child should see," he whispered.

"I still want to go," she said.

He looked at her for a long time and finally sighed. "Let's pack."

"I'm going?"

"You said you're brave enough to write the truth. We'll see," he said.

She looked at him, trying to see behind his eyes, trying to feel his truth, but she could only feel his hand in hers and there were no words to capture her spirit.

"When do we leave?" she said finally.

"Now," he said. "We leave now."

CHAPTER THIRTEEN

*T*he big green National Guard tent was set up just off the Nolichucky close to the main highway and was the center of all search activities. Hundreds of volunteers gathered around the tent, and vehicles were stacked like parking at a traveling circus. The trail led up from the site into the mountains and all below gazed upward and in it, like the trail itself was a channel to a distant dimension of death and horror, holding the spirits of the murderous and the lost tightly within its innards, holding fast to the contents of their concern.

Occasionally, a search crew would come down

the mountain and file into the tent for food and coffee and all would gather around asking news of the girl and the bear and there began stories of things unheard of in those mountains of Tennessee, fears founded in things unnatural and of some different spirit. A people who lived there and had lived there for generations, who had never taken to things unfamiliar or foreign, were now bound by the intrusion and could not remove it. Their desire to find Anna, dead or alive, stemmed from something inherently good within them, those feelings that all people share for the innocent and young. To them the bear, this foreign spirit of death and evil, was the kidnapper of their highlander security and must be destroyed. Their human spirits soared.

There was a smaller tent closer to the river roped off from the rest. The sheriff sat inside drinking coffee studying a map. His radio crackled in low volume, staticky words of his men following their orders to return to base. He worked the map with a red pen, marking those areas searched and those yet to be explored, signs of the bear, and possible routes of escape the girl may have used. It all added up to nothing. In frustration he swallowed the last gulp from the cup as the door to the tent cracked and a deputy's head poked in.

"The youngun's kin is hy'ar," he said.

The sheriff looked straight ahead without blinking and nodded as the tent door opened wider allowing an old man to enter. The man moved toward the sheriff and extended his hand.

"I'm Warner Roby," he said. "Anna's grandfather."

"Mr. Roby, name's Hicks."

"So," the old man said nervously. "Any progress?"

"Pull up a seat, Mr. Roby. Would you care for coffee?"

"No thank you," he said.

"Mr. Roby, I have men up on that mountain and we're lookin' hard for the child, but we've found nothin' yet. And that could be good, for if she was in a bad way, we would have probably found her."

"You mean if she were dead?" asked the grandfather.

"Yessir."

"She's not dead, Sheriff."

"I understand. A soul needs to keep the faith for the best."

"I always keep the faith, Sheriff, but my knowledge of her condition is much deeper than my faith."

The sheriff looked at the old man in an

uncomfortable pause. "What knowledge is that?"

Warner Roby smiled. "That's personal."

"Personal?"

"Yes sir. It is. Is Mr. Shaw here yet?"

"What?"

"Adam Shaw," Roby said. "He's supposed to meet me here this morning."

The sheriff stood, his face flushed and jerking. "I garntee that Shaw will not be discoverin' this child any quicker'n two hunerd of my men. He's a wizard, Mr. Roby. A freak of sarcumstance with the luck of the devil hisself. It ain't right the way the man can find things. You should be fearful his spirit will be close to your youngin."

"What I fear, Sheriff, is whatever is killing people up there, not Mr. Shaw's spirit," said the grandfather calmly.

"Mr. Roby, I need to know if you have information 'bout the child's condition, even if you think it's personal."

Warner Roby looked seriously at the man across the table. "She's alive. She's terribly lost with no hint of a safe way home. She's battling fear, Sheriff. It is a great war for her but she's holding on. Annu is a gutsy child."

"How do you know these things?"

The old man smiled again. "When you get as

old as me, maybe you'll know some things too."

"Have you talked to someone who has seen her?"

"No sir," he said looking straight at the sheriff. "A message from her."

"A message?" the sheriff prodded.

"Do you hear the words of your Father in Heaven, Sheriff?"

The sheriff smiled. "You mean like Moses in the movie? No," he said.

"This isn't a movie," the old man said.

"And this young'un ain't God, Mr. Roby."

"I agree," he smiled. "But they're pretty good friends."

*   *   *

Micah felt uneasy about the silence and whispers and heads turning. She heard "that's him" and "he's here" as Adam passed through the crowd of people toward the tent like some big brother who just arrived to vindicate a sibling. She followed behind him enclosed in their views and her uneasiness gave way to a strange pride of association and she lifted her head and walked faster, catching up and taking her space beside him. Glancing up at his face she detected a concentration that made her pause, an intensity of some force unknown to her, so she looked away.

From the crowd six men emerged from different directions, some older, some younger than
the Finder, and they took the space around
Adam and Micah without speaking, walking
with them, their eyes searching ahead and in the
crowd. Micah looked at them nervously and
then at Adam, searching for some clue as to their
purpose, but she detected nothing except an
acceptance of each other's presence. Her eyes
quickly found bulges in their waistbands, a dark
handled Colt under a flopping jacket and she
was suddenly fearful of the next moments.

Three deputies blocked their path at the small
tent. "Can we help you?" said one.

"I'm looking for Mr. Roby," said the Finder.

The six men eased away encircling the deputies.
"Whoa, here boys, what you think yor doin'," the
deputy said. "You bunch of damn game wardens.
You boys wanna dance or somethin'?"

The sheriff emerged from the tent with the old
man and stood red-faced in front of the tent.
There was no sound. No talking. All eyes
watched. His eyes were on the Finder. "I don't
remember sending you no invitation," he whispered across the space.

"I've come to see Mr. Roby," Adam said.

The sheriff moved toward the Finder, parting the men in front of him. "The great Finder! You make me sick! Plantin' all your seeds of doubt amonst folks, that there's some witchery to findin' lost souls."

"No witches here, Sheriff," Adam said.

"Oh yeah. From what I just heard, I'd say there's witchery and the devil hisself and his name is Adam Shaw."

"I'm no devil. Just read sign most folks miss."

"You offend me. This here is my county. My people. They come to me for help. Nobody here asked for you. You scare the hell out of me with your ways. You scare my people."

"Your people?"

"My people!" yelled the sheriff.

"This girl that's lost. Is she your people?" asked Adam.

"Anybody that's in my county is mine. You included, Shaw. Your future is in my hands. And the girl … she'll be found, dead or alive, by my people or not at all. You got it, Buddy?" He punched Adam Shaw on the chest with his finger for emphasis.

The Finder's strike was so hard and fast that people stood awestruck. The sheriff stood in disbelief, holding his damaged arm. A deputy's hand went to his gun, but a game warden's stern grip stopped his movement. "We didn't come here to fight," Adam said. "I won't stand for your lies. I can't abide your bullying. If I die here right now, so be it."

"I'll hang your damned … "

"Stop it," the Finder said. "Stop your filthy mouth." The sheriff stood glassy-eyed.

"Arrest this son of a bitch," he said to his men. He looked around him for support, but they dropped their heads in response. "I said arrest him!"

The Finder turned to the crowd. "Does anyone have fault with me finding this child? Anyone, except this man!"

The crowd responded, "NO!" Their voices echoed off the mountain and fell back on them.

When Adam turned to the sheriff, the man was stern-faced and everyone looked at him. There was a silence that fell over the people and the Finder said so all could hear: "This is not about us, you and me." He waited as the sheriff looked back at him. "I'm askin'," Adam said.

The sheriff turned without speaking and disappeared into the tent. Adam addressed the old man. "Mr. Roby," he said. The old man extended his hand in greeting and they moved off through the crowd. Adam stopped briefly and searched for Micah.

She stood looking at him from the crowd and he motioned to her, but she did not move, and they stared at each other for a long time. She watched as they gathered, the brother game wardens, and they all turned toward her as if they would not leave without her. She sighed and moved forward and the security of their brotherhood embraced her as she walked.

"Boys, I appreciate it," the Finder said to his friends and one of them said no problem and they dispersed back into the crowd and were gone, leaving whisperings and stories building behind them.

CHAPTER FOURTEEN

L ike some chess game on a greater plane, the
pieces moved, their futures not ordained by
the hand that guided them, but by the simple color
of themselves, white or black. The purpose of the
engagement was somehow tied to the purity of
their color, for there were many chameleons on the
board, shifting colors as they moved, so that it was
difficult to determine adversaries. The changing
colors of the pieces became important in themselves, not that they would be immediately
removed from the game, but alter their allegiance
prior to being taken. The glaring observation on
the board became those pieces that rarely changed,

remaining whiter or blacker as time progressed and there was a gathering of others around them, drawn to their purity and the color in itself had strength. The hearts of the living pieces directed the contest, its direction, its purpose, and the board was tremendous in size and scope but unimportant in the end. A contest on one board that led to another and it played on both planes simultaneously, and yet only a few warriors understood and they were the pieces that remained pure in their color with faith that someday they would finally see the players. It was Adam Shaw's greatest fear, his greatest struggle. In order to find the truth, he must brush closely to the other color, understand it, embrace it, but he could not change himself. He could not change colors. To do so would remove his ability to see the second board. Reading sign was his gift, it took all his concentration and will to use his gift on both boards.

*   *   *

Leaving the crowd at the tents, they drove a short distance down a graveled road that remained damp from the fast-moving creek alongside. They stopped at a pull-over and gathered near a large hemlock that overhung the water. Warner Roby looked up into the mountain above, its silence moving him and he shuddered once before turning to Adam and Micah. "The mountain. It's powerful," he said.

"Yessir," the Finder whispered.

"She is the most ... " and his voice broke. He cleared his throat and began again. "I wish you knew her."

"Do you have a picture? I'd like to know what she looks like."

The old man smiled and returned to his car, emerging with a picture and his eyes couldn't leave the photo and Micah touched his shoulder in sympathy. Adam took the picture and stared into it and then he turned away. He left them and walked across the road and into the timber and was gone for several minutes and they stood there waiting for something to happen that would explain, but when he returned he was somber offering no clue.

"Thank you," he said handing back the picture.

"She is alive," the grandfather said.

The sound of the water surrounded them and Micah backed away leaning on the truck watching the two as they talked. For a brief moment she thought she could actually see the emotion between them, their eyes holding tight in the center of it, like an almost visible vapor of humanity clinging to the river's sound around them. She studied Adam's face and the depth of it amazed her. His intensity was in the blueness of the eyes and the small wrinkles at their edges, the way his lips moved when he talked, never jerky or drastic, but fluid and the voice that emerged was deep and clear and gentle. "Tell me about her," he said.

The old man paused. "She was orphaned when she was three. My daughter and her husband were missionaries in Rwanda ... they got caught up in some revolution. It's hard for me to understand the wars over there. Soldiers found Anna in the room where her parents were murdered. She was praying when they found her. At three, Mr. Shaw. She was praying on her knees. They found six others, rebels, dead in the room. Not a mark on them, their bloody knives still in their hands, but dead all around her."

"What are you saying?" Adam asked.

"Other things have happened since she came to live with me. She has tried real hard to be a normal little girl, but she's not. When you find her you'll see. She can be just like any girl one minute and the next is like talking to someone very old and wise. Her wisdom ages her. There are those who are afraid of the things she knows." He walked a few steps away from Adam, staring up into the loneliness of the mountains above them. "There seems to be a darkness that follows her, but ... this," he said, "is beyond me. She is alone and lost and that animal is up there with her, looking for her."

Adam looked at him. "Following her?"

"As I said, the darkness follows her. You are in great danger if you go up there," the old man said.

Adam smiled. "But that's where I'll find Anna."

"Don't let this young lady go," the old man said.

Adam looked at Micah. "She goes her own way."

"And what way is that?" asked the old man of Micah. "Tell me."

"Mr. Roby. I'll be fine. I've hiked every mountain range in North America and most in Europe. I'll be okay."

"You see," he said to Adam. "She has no idea." He turned to Micah again. "Why would you go?"

"Adam will find your granddaughter," she said. "And I'll be there."

The grandfather of the lost girl studied Micah without talking.

"We should go," Adam said. "But I need a favor before we leave."

"What?"

"Pray for us," Adam smiled.

The old man paused. "She told me about a dream," he whispered. "I didn't want her to go on this trip but she said she had a dream and there was this man, a woodsman she said, who would protect her."

The creek sounded around them. "You can help," Adam said.

The old man looked at the ground, then at Micah and changed direction. "How do you find the lost?" he asked. "Like the sheriff said, hundreds have searched."

"How did those men die … the ones who killed her parents?"

"I don't know," said the old man.

"But you believe you know," said Adam.

"She is loved that much," the old man said.

"That's a powerful thought," Adam said.

Micah looked at the Finder over the old man's shoulder.

"We all are," Adam said to Micah. "I'll venture the child just believes it a might more than the rest of us."

*   *   *

They turned onto a dim road and drove another mile deeper into the mountain, sloshing mud and branches scraped against the windshield.

"We'll leave the truck here. We can cut straight across there and hit the main trail." He moved the seat forward and removed a holstered revolver and a short-barreled Remington pump shotgun. Adam belted on the revolver and then slung on a large backpack and strapped in. Micah was ready when he finished, her pack seeming entirely too large for her frame. "Can you carry that?" he asked.

"I could carry you," she said. "It's all in the legs."

Adam smiled. "I doubt if they're big enough," he said moving away. She took a deep breath. "Let's go," she said, "and I won't even ask about the guns." Adam started walking and her words stopped him. "Okay, I lied. What are the guns for? The bear?"

"I doubt if they're big enough," he said moving away again and she followed.

They made a mile quickly. The trail he made was very steep and she was only breathing slightly when they topped out on the main trail. "How old are you?" she asked.

"A lot older'n you," he teased.

"For an older man, you cut an impressive trail," she said smiling.

"You're not so bad, yourself," he said.

"Where now?" Micah asked.

"It's about three miles to Curly Maple Gap. The attack took place at Cherry Gap another twelve miles. I'd like to make it before dark."

"Fifteen miles in," she looked at her watch, "eight hours?"

"About," he said.

She shook her head. "Let's try it."

They started again, this time with a different pace, but the trail was comfortable under her feet as she matched his stride. Micah thought about many things while she walked behind him, like what his eyes saw and of Anna somewhere out there, maybe, though she would not allow herself to think of the bear, because it made her lose her breath and caused her heart to beat differently. They passed through tremendous thickets of rhododendron and hemlocks and the air was still and the woods were very quiet around them, except for the ethereal music of veeries and wood thrushes. At Curly Maple Gap they rested, lowering their packs and sitting against the lean-to. Micah was sweating as she took her first drink of water. "Talk to me," she said. "I need you to talk to me."

He rested the Remington against the lean-to wall and drank from her canteen when she offered it. "What do you want to know?"

"How are you?" she smiled.

He looked at her as if the question was foreign to him — in some different language.

"I need to know you are okay," she said. "When you enter that secret world of yours, I feel alone." He just looked at her. "What?" she asked.

"You said you were brave."

"Look," she said, "I'm here. Right here on this mountain with you."

"Do you believe I tell the truth?" he asked.

"Yes. I do."

Adam sighed and then began. "People leave parts of themselves behind when they move. Dogs can smell it. I see it."

She paused looking at him, trying not to show her feelings, believing him to be sincere, but knowing the strangeness of his words. "What do you see?" she asked. He took her finger and guiding it down, touched the soil at the trail's edge, then lifted it away and stared at the ground where she had touched. "Colors," he whispered. She stared into his face, his eyes looking down at the ground. "Okay. What have you seen so far?" she asked.

"Maybe a hundred people have moved down this trail. It's confusing. I'm hoping that when we reach the attack site the sign will change."

"Why would it change there?" she asked.

"Fear," he said. "It changes everything. It separates the sign."

They sat there in the silence of the mountainside and said nothing for a long time. "You want me to be honest with you, right?" she said cautiously.

"Yes."

"The sheriff called you a witch or wizard or something," she said. "You tell me about seeing colors where people walk. Does he know about the colors? Is that why he called you the name?"

"I've never told another living soul, except you. He just knows I have found people that were beyond being found," Adam laughed, "and now you think I'm a wizard."

"No! I don't! I'm just trying to understand all this. It's difficult."

"I know. It's hard to understand how some kid can play Mozart at five, but it happens," he said.

"How long have you been able to do this?"

"I was twenty-seven the first time it happened," Adam said. "I'm told there is a medical term for it. Extremely rare, they say. Synesthesia, or something like that."

"That's different than a child born with God-given talent," she said.

"You're right. It's different. And exactly the same."

"What's the difference?" she asked.

"Twenty-two years."

"And you think it's the same?"

"Its purpose is the same," Adam replied.

"You're worried that I think you're crazy, aren't you?"

"Interested, not worried."

"I may think your gift is wonderful," Micah offered.

"No, you don't," he said.

"Don't tell me what I think," she said standing. "It pisses me off."

They moved without talking, Micah following behind and watching, wondering as she stepped lightly what colors lay before his eyes, how long the colors lasted. More than anything she wondered about the color of her own steps. Sometimes Adam would stop and stand there looking down at the trail, his head seeking this way and that, up the trail and then into the woods, almost as if he was listening for some voice of direction, and then, without emotion, he would continue on as if nothing was learned. She wanted desperately to continue her questions, but considering his mood, thought better of it and kept to herself.

They reached Cherry Gap at dusk. She was tired and drenched in sweat and glad to be rid of the weight of her pack. She watched as Adam stowed his gear and immediately began gathering wood for a fire, stacking it in a pile by the lean-to. Micah wondered how he could do that because she was totally exhausted, her muscles aching from the hike. He started the fire gradually in the fire pit, feeding it match-sized twigs, long and twisty, which flared up suddenly in the smoke and crackling, and then broken pieces of wood the size of her fingers and then her wrists and finally her legs until the fire was established sprouting flames, the heat moving the tree branches above them like some spirit-shrub rooted in living glowing coals. Adam watched the center of the fire for a moment, focused sleepy-eyed, captivated by its primitive pull.

Adam shook himself out of his revelry. "I'm gonna look around," he said. "Stay by the fire," and he was gone, his footsteps receding from her one by one into the mountain's dusk. Micah did not move until blackness overtook the space outside the fire and then she added some of the wood that Adam had piled high next to the shelter. She stood at the edge of the light, in that dimension where the flames cast their glow the

Gary Cook

farthest before giving way to the consuming blackness. She thought about supper and what they might eat. She was starved. It was then that she heard him call.

She moved toward the sound of his voice, step by step in the darkness through tree branches that scratched her face, her feet finding their way and she was terribly afraid of the darkness but bound to close the distance. Finally she stood next to him. "What did you find?" she whispered.

He did not speak for a long time. "Look," he said kneeling down in the leaves. "Can you see it?"

She hesitated and then said truthfully. "What, Adam?"

"Her print. It's so plain and I've never seen that color. Never."

She knelt beside him. "I can't. I'm sorry," she whispered.

"Look!" he said. "Here ... here ... here," he said moving away from her in the darkness following the spoor.

"Adam!" she yelled. "Don't leave me." She felt his grip on her arm and he pulled her deeper into the woods.

"C'mon," he said.

"It's too dark. I can't see."

"Tuck your fingers into my belt. Follow me,"

he ordered.

She followed like some mindless caboose, winding through the timber and darkness while Adam sought Anna's path and direction. If Micah had doubts before about his ability to see the unseen, they left her now. His path was as purposeful as Anna's had been fearful and uncertain. Micah could feel the sense of panic in Anna's lack of direction. She tried to put out of her mind the conditions of the night, of the attack, the rain and lightning, the wind, darkness, blood, death, and the bear.

An hour later they returned to camp, leaving Anna's trail reluctantly, but the mountain was difficult at night and although Adam could see her tracks, the night was still very black and he was concerned about Micah. They sat at the fire's edge, eating slowly and staring into its glow. "Could you see the bear's track?" she asked.

"No, I can't. No animals. Only man."

"Why not?"

"I have a theory," he said.

"And …"

"Animals lack human souls, they are of this world only, but man's immortality is in another world. We don't really die. It's when the soul has a physical body that it leaves sign here."

"That doesn't sound like a medical condition," Micah said.

"I ask for answers. Sometimes I get them," he said.

"Is that what your life's about, Adam? Finding answers?"

"More about finding the strength to ask the right questions," he said.

"I think that life is about being happy, trying to find happiness, searching for it," she said.

"Like I said ... "

"But you don't seem happy. I wish I could see you happy," she smiled.

"Stick around," he said. "I'm working on it."

Micah stood and walked to him, standing in front of him, blocking him from the fire. "Your eyes ... sometimes they talk to me," she said.

"They've always been blabby like that." He smiled. "Can't seem to do much about it."

They stepped into the firelight from the darkness, three men in dirty denims, staying at the edge of the darkness so that the light flickered off their faces. Micah saw them and gasped, jumping backwards. Two of them held shotguns with taped forearms and battered stocks and Adam was now standing between the approaching men and Micah, the firelight surrounding him like some golden halo.

"How you boys doing?" Adam said.

"We'uns doin' fine. Real fine," said their leader.

"I'll give you this … you don't make much noise," Adam continued.

"Looks to us like you war studyin' the girl's eyes. Warn't thinkin' much about hearin' nothin'. Move away there, boy. Let's have a looksee at the girl."

"Put the guns down. We'll talk about it," Adam said.

Micah's knees were unsteady as she moved toward Adam. He extended his arm behind him as she neared, touching her, keeping her behind him, never taking his eyes from the men.

"Whoo damn!" said one of the men moving sideways. "Lookee har!" He laughed and Micah could see the gaps in his mouth where teeth once lived and he extended the gun in front of him, using the barrel as a pointer, stepping closer to her. The barrel inched forward toward her breast and he followed the barrel with his eyes, breathing through his mouth, the tongue protruding slightly. She instinctively moved back.

"Don't you move, girly. Stay put," he said.

Adam watched the man's right hand, the finger on the trigger, as the barrel came again. "Stop it," Adam said. "Look at me." The man looked up.

"Stop it. Now!"

"Hell no, you soma bitch. I wanna play with her. And you ain't gonna do shit, you hear me. Maybe I'll let you watch, boy. How's that?"

Adam's gun came from his holster, forcing the man to swing the shotgun in defense, but he was late and the revolver was between his eyes. Micah gasped again, stepping backwards.

"Wait!" yelled the man without a gun, stepping into the light, his companion beside him with a shotgun pointed at the Finder. "Study on it, Game Wardener. You kill him. He kills you. That leaves me and Old Bunk here with the girl and all night to do it."

Micah's heart hurt, beating so hard she thought maybe she was having a heart attack and then she thought that was good, urging it on.

"What do you want?" asked Adam.

"Sheriff sent us on a bear hunt of sorts. We wanna be heroes."

"I see … well … here's how it's gonna go. You can turn around and leave and it's all forgotten. Do it now."

"Or what?" the leader grinned.

"Or try to kill me and try to take the girl. You're big boys. Make your own road. Choose wrong and you die, but you will not have her.

You remember that."

"Hell, we're all gonna die," he laughed. "I'll go out smilin'," the leader said and quickly grabbed Micah's shirt collar, ripping it open. She stood exposed, quivering in the firelight, facing Adam. The three hollered in delight at her nakedness.

"Micah! Look at me!" Adam yelled above their voices. "No fear. None. Micah! Look at me!" Adam Shaw tried to fight all his training to kill the man in front of him and try the others, but his finger began its pull on the trigger anyway.

"Old Bunk," said the leader, "kill him. Blow the bastard's head off." And Old Bunk moved closer with the shotgun pointing it at the Finder's head. Micah kept her eyes on Adam and she saw in them a resolve as he slowly lowered his gun.

"Don't watch," the Finder said to her. "Shut your eyes." Micah shut her eyes. She heard a painful scream and a sickening thud and a gunshot and a man yelling in fear and quick footsteps in the leaves and a gasping, gurgling for air. She still felt Adam's arms around her, holding her close. What was happening? Who was fighting? She heard Adam's whispered words in her ear, "keep them shut." The gasping continued, but not as loud and then it ended and all was quiet. Adam retrieved a blanket from his pack and placed it around her and she opened her eyes and tried to turn to see but he stopped her.

"Who are you?" Adam said to the darkness.

"A friend," came a deep voice. The stranger walked slowly around the fire to the shelter and sat on a stump at fire's edge.

"Are you okay?" Adam whispered to her. Her eyes stayed on the stranger, dark skinned and long black hair. He wore jeans and a cut-off sweatshirt. A leather belt held the sheaths of a large knife and a hatchet. He looked at them across the fire, breathing easily.

"I'm okay. Are we okay?" she said.

"Sit down. Don't look behind you," Adam said. They stared back across the fire at the stranger.

"Do you have water?" the stranger asked. Adam went to his pack and handed the stranger a canteen. He washed his hands and face and then he drank.

"Thank you," he said.

"Who are you?" Adam asked.

The stranger looked at him with surprise. "You don't know?"

"No," Adam said.

"I am your brother from the heart of the land," he motioned with hand signals.

"Heart of the land?"

"Yes."

"What people?" Adam asked.

"I serve the Apache."

The Finder paused. "And you know me?"

"You are the Spirit Tracker. The one who sees Spirit Sign."

Micah looked at Adam as the words hit him, so she moved to him and stood behind him and placed her hands on his back. "No one knows that," Adam said.

"You are the finder of the Daughter Who Sees. You have been foretold."

"The Daughter Who Sees?" Adam questioned.

"Yes, the one you call Anna."

They listened to the fire for a long time. "What about these men?" Micah asked, looking quickly behind her, noticing no marks of violence on them.

"Do not gaze upon them. They are dead," he said across the fire. "And the dirty one … he did not die with a smile on his face."

"Does it harm you to kill?" the Finder asked.

"They killed themselves … by their own actions." The fire popped, sending sparks in flight. "What would you have done, if you had not seen me?" the stranger continued.

"I did see you," Adam said.

"I thought you could not kill another man, not

even to protect yourself, but I believe you were close to killing," the stranger said.

"I could, but I would lose my way," Adam said.

"To track this girl's spirit?"

"Yes," Adam said.

"I understand. Then life is as it should be."

"It is difficult to be true to both worlds," Adam said.

"At first, but over time, you will see it becomes easier."

"How?" the Finder asked.

"There is only one world. Others are but learning grounds, if the spirit wishes to continue."

"I would like it to be easier," Adam said.

"I think you should pray more," the stranger said.

"I'll work on that," Adam said. "To whom should I pray?"

He smiled. "You test me, but that is understandable. The one God."

"And Jesus?" asked the Finder.

"Jesus is the Father, but then you know that, and the idea of the Father, a good loving Father who always protects His children so long as they wish His protection and guidance is the greatest truth of your people."

The Finder smiled.

"Now, Brother. You show me how to read spirit sign," the stranger said.

The Finder tossed a small limb into the fire and watched it ignite. "You tell me who you are, first."

"I am your friend. I help you in certain matters. That is all you must believe, if you wish. But it is your choice to believe or not believe."

"It's the same reading spirit sign. I can't teach you something that is not of me," said the Finder.

The stranger smiled. "The fire is dying. You should build it again and I will take care of those men behind us in the darkness."

"Their deaths must be reported. It's my law," the Finder said.

"Your law is not here, my Brother. A greater law is in place. I will take care of these men. They will be comforted, if they desire. Their deaths are not on your heart."

"But they are dead," Micah said. "How can they be comforted?"

The stranger looked at her. "They are dead to this world. Our Father finds goodness where we may not see, and His compassion is great for His children, even the foolish." He left the fire and disappeared into the darkness and they heard him dragging their bodies through the leaves. Micah and Adam watched the fire for a long time before speaking. "What's happening to us?" she asked.

"I'm not sure," he said.

"Will he be back?"

"I don't have a clue." he said.

CHAPTER FIFTEEN

*T*he stranger returned a long time later. They never heard him. He just appeared at the edge of the firelight. Micah studied him as he moved closer, thinking him beautiful like some animal perfect in movement.

"What is your name?" she said.

He stopped, looking at her across the fire. "You could not say it right if I told you," he said.

"Wanna bet," she said.

"Jack. You can call me Jack."

"That's not Indian."

"What is in a name except to be remembered by?"

She watched him for a second. "How did you

get here?"

He sat in the leaves at the fire's edge. "I drove an old truck to Oklahoma until it died. Got a ride with a preacher from Tennessee to Nashville. Took a bus to Knoxville. Rode a motorcycle to the mountain."

"A motorcycle?"

"Yes," he said. "A Harley. It was very loud."

Micah looked at Adam and then back across the fire. "Are you hungry?" Adam asked.

"I have not eaten in three days. Yes."

Adam went to his pack and produced a supper, but Jack ate slowly, not like a man starving. "Where did you start?" Adam asked.

"Start?"

"You said you drove to Oklahoma. From where?"

"The mountains ... southwest of Oklahoma. You would also have trouble saying the mountain's name if I told you."

"Are you alone?" asked Adam.

Jack looked around him. "Yes, I believe so. But many are coming."

"I don't understand ... many," Adam said.

"I would not think I was the only one who was guided here, but if so, that is as it is. You must forgive me. This is new for us, too. It has been a long time since we were given the authority to speak to you."

"Why not?" Micah asked.

"That is complicated."

"Why now?" Micah continued.

"The moon has turned. It has been foretold."

Micah looked up. The sky was dark.

"Ask something else," Jack said.

"Would you tell me about the girl?" Micah said. "What is her place among your people?"

"My people? She is for all people … but I do not understand it completely. She will comfort many in times ahead. She sings a song of connection to the Father."

"A song?" she asked.

"What is it about music that touches your soul and makes tears or causes your body to dance? What is it about notes of song or string that holds a person?" Jack asked.

"There's good music and evil music," Adam said. "It's very strong."

"Her song is good, my Brother. She will touch us as the sunset stops our thoughts or the sound of geese passing overhead makes you ponder their spirit. These things are from the source of life — so is her song. It comes from the beginning of life and passes through our hearts to the end of life and we are touched by its path. It is like a baby looking deeply into the eyes of its mother, knowing nothing of motherhood, but feeling all that is good about mothers."

A breeze moved the fire's flames and the leaves rustled high in the trees above them and then it was still again. The Indian looked behind them, his eyes focused on the sky at the horizon above the trees. "The wounded moon. It is rising," he said.

They turned and above the land's darker line a crimson moon was partially visible, fully rounded in its definition, staring at them like some angry, red eye of heaven. "I've never seen the moon like that before," Micah said. They turned and his eyes sparkled in the firelight, glistening wet as he stared into the sky. "What causes the moon to turn red?" she asked.

"As I said, the moon is wounded."

He lowered the food and stood. "I must go. You must know, Brother, I cannot protect you from the bear. He has done nothing wrong. The violence in him is not of his doing. He is tainted by darkness ... like the land is poisoned by people."

The Finder stood. "Please. Don't go. I need your help. Is the bear after the girl?"

"Yes."

"Why?"

"So many questions."

"I have many more," Adam said.

"Is goodness not always vulnerable to violence?" Jack asked.

"Yes, but why would the bear want her?" Adam asked.

"Perhaps darkness loves the light, seeks its goodness, but it cannot do other than be itself."

"I don't believe that a bear has such thoughts or becomes dark," Adam said.

"He doesn't," said Jack. "He is driven, as all life is powered by things greater."

"What if the bear kills the girl?" asked Micah.

"You are a girl. What if the bear kills you?" he asked.

Micah paused. "Then I'll die."

Jack turned back to Adam. "Then people will have killed her through this great bear and my Brother has not fulfilled his vision."

"What will you do then?" Micah asked.

Jack shrugged. "Maybe I will see if the Harley lives long enough to get me home."

*   *   *

Later when the stranger was gone, they lay in their sleeping bags at the fire's edge and stared up into the stars, the wounded moon rising. Micah was lost in the sky, wanting to escape the depth, but strangely held by its pull. Finally, she turned her head toward him. His eyes were open, catching the flickering of the fire in their sight. "What are you thinking?" she whispered. "What does it mean?" she asked.

"I'm trying real hard to figure it out," he whispered. They were quiet for a while and then he continued. "Do you pray?" he asked.

She looked at him and turned her eyes back to the sky. "Like most people, I guess. Sometimes. When I was little, I prayed that my dog would not die. He did. I prayed that my father would get well. He didn't. I prayed that my mom wouldn't marry her new bastard lover. She did. Then I prayed that he would die and he didn't. I guess I'm doing something wrong."

"I don't know anything about your past," he said. "It feels like we've known each other for a long time, but I ... "

"You never pry," she said.

"What was your dog's name?" he asked.

"Scout," she said. "That dog loved me so much."

"That's the thing about dogs," he said. "The devotion. They are the best of all the friends and family and lovers all rolled into one bag of fur."

"My father gave me the dog. I guess that made it more special," she whispered.

Adam rolled to his side, facing her. "Tell me about your father."

She looked at him, and then rolled to face him, so that their words were only whispers between them.

"I was an only child. He doted after me."

"Doted?"

"Yes. He spoiled me with attention. In Tennessee talk, he fussed over me."

"What's the best thing your father ever gave you … I mean, besides the doting thing?"

She smiled. "He gave me assurance that I could do anything. He was so positive. He would get really upset if I gave any clue that I was hesitant to tackle anything."

"What was his name?" Adam asked.

"Philip," she said. "His name was Philip; he raised me in Vermont, in the country, and I was the biggest tomboy you ever saw."

"And your mom?"

Micah looked down, and then back up into his eyes. "I just as soon not talk about her. If it's okay," she said.

"It's okay, Micah. Everything is gonna be okay."

"How do you pray?" she asked. She saw his hand in front of her eyes, strong and steady. She took it.

"First," he said, "shut your eyes."

She did. The night became alive with sound, louder than she ever remembered, but it was a blending of night sounds, the chorus of frogs and crickets, peepers and owls, becoming one with her feelings of the deep sky above her. He whispered. "Just listen."

She smiled, keeping her eyes shut, and in that period of meditation, above the sounds of the night, she heard the first notes. They were mysteriously clear, but very far away, a singing of notes so pleading in its melody that she felt a great pain in her heart. For a moment Micah thought she had fallen asleep and was dreaming like in those deep-sleep dreams where emotion holds the spirit and an entire existence is spun around that emotion. She opened her eyes, willing the sleep to stop and the song to cease and the pain in her heart to subside, but it did not.

She saw Adam standing above her, his eyes searching the darkness in the direction of the singing. The song was not kin to any human expression they had ever heard and its power stopped the sounds of nature, echoing in that wilderness vastness, a melodic voice of solitude and fear, a lonely, wordless beckoning for something good in the darkness.

Adam fell to his knees and Micah reached for his hand, holding it tightly as they listened, the song continuing like some great overture of emotion, and in that time they felt the source of all great composers past and poets future, the beginnings of human pain and separation, the yearning for compassion. Adam and Micah felt all of these things in the blackness of that mountain night in the voice of the lost girl, Anna, who sang in her solitude toward the heavens. The song stopped. There was total silence. No insects or birds of the night spoke. "What was that?" she asked.

"It was Anna ... "

A roar interrupted his words. It came from the same direction as the song before, these notes of a different source, deep-throated and with great feeling — mixed with coughs and contortions of some horrible pain, but not human. With these echoes rode the power of its source, an airborne concert of madness, confusion and determination that filled the space around them like some odor of fear and left them holding each other at the fire's edge. The maddening roars continued for a full minute and then faded away, leaving the mountain intensely quiet again.

"My God," she whispered.

"That's like no bear I've ever heard," he whispered.

"What's happening here?" she asked.

"War, I think," he said. "Maybe a strange war."

CHAPTER SIXTEEN

S he watched him packing their gear in dawn's light. Holding a small flashlight in her mouth, she wrote in her journal:

May 2: *In spite of all that has happened, I dreamed about Adam last night. We talked for hours and he was not the same. It was as if this great burden had been lifted from him and we were normal. There was no bear, no fear of death, no mystery other than our eyes. I told him about my theory of the Melungeons and we made love on his front porch. I have never felt what I felt in that dream, not in reality have I ever felt such passion,* *such gentleness, such a desire to be loved that I felt in that dream. I have never felt so needed. I have never given myself so completely. I have never known what making love was until last night. My hands still tremble ...*

In ten minutes they were moving, covering ground very fast that had been shrouded in darkness the night before. The mountain was eerie in its dawning mask, its shapes and features blending into a mountain being, alive with the sounds it had spawned the night before. Micah followed as before but now she saw Adam work the track with a greater purpose, showing an intense awareness of the space in front of them. He carried the shotgun as if it were an extension of himself. She marveled at the way he moved it in and out of the brush they penetrated, his eyes always moving from the ground and up again and sometimes behind them. Once he had whispered quickly, "Stay close."

There was no purposeful direction in Anna's track, just movement until they crested a ridge. It seemed once on the top, she embraced the elevation, able to feel in the darkness when she strayed from its line. Every time her trail led off the crest she would quickly turn back up before continuing. Eventually the ridge crest fell and she followed it, descending steeply to the black hollow below where she made large circles in her lost course, finding nothing that provided safety. Adam visualized her trying desperately to move away from something terrible behind her, and yet wondering if it could be just ahead in the darkness.

Adam stopped abruptly. Micah moved beside him looking into the dense green underbrush. A thrush called beside them. The forest canopy was cathedral-like, the shafting light like a stained-glass window from heaven through the leaves of trees monumental and ancient. "What?" she asked nervously.

"There," he whispered, pointing with his eyes through the greenness. A piece of cloth, torn with ragged edges, hung from a branch of rhododendron. Micah moved forward. "No," he said pulling her back. "You smell it?" She tried the air, drawing it inside of her, a sweet-soured musky scent that was strangely attractive. She looked at him and mouthed the words ... "What is it?"

"Stay here," he mouthed back. "No," she shook her head with emphasis. He paused and then motioned for her to stay behind him. Parting the limbs with the barrel of the shotgun he moved forward, their footfalls crunching quietly in the leaves. They stood before the piece of purple cloth, ragged in its edges, bloodless in color, a part of her left behind. The ground around them was disturbed, smelling freshly of its mountain soul, moist darkness torn from beneath by claws and teeth and the smell of its source that had rolled like some relentless dog in an attempt to get closer to her scent.

There was no sign of Anna, other than the purple cloth draping over a limb. There was no blood or flesh or clue of attack, just sign of wallowing in her scent. Adam retrieved the cloth, fingered it delicately and passed it to Micah before leaving the spot following some invisible sign of Anna deeper into the understory.

After making a large circle they topped the main ridge two hours later looking up and down the Appalachian Trail, its presence so different than the trail they had just followed, clear and distinct, with direction and purpose. They knelt in the trail, shoulder to shoulder. "What did she do?" Micah asked.

"She crossed it." His eyes showed the way of her footsteps leading into the timber on the other side of the trail and for the first time Micah saw a physical track, a tennis shoe with wavy lines in its soul, pressed in the soil at the trail's edge. She looked up at him. "You are real," she whispered to herself. Adam studied the trail, looking intensely at the bare ground beneath them. "What?" she asked softly.

"We have company," he said. "One man."

"Could it be Jack?" she said looking for the man track, but seeing nothing.

"No," he said. "Jack's sign is not the color of man."

"What?"

Adam turned to her, smiled briefly, and whispered. "See it, Micah. Open your eyes to what's happening."

"Jack's not real?"

"He is very real," he said. "You saw him. Don't you believe your own eyes?"

Micah looked at him with frustration. "You're pissing me off, Adam. Don't play with me anymore. Just tell me what you know."

"I know you're looking at the greatest story a writer ever witnessed and you're angry at me. You should be happy." He smiled again. "C'mon."

"No," she said flatly. "Tell me about Jack."

"We don't have time."

"How much time will it take?"

"Come or stay. It's your choice," he said.

Adam saw the man first, standing in the trail watching them and then Micah stared too. "He's backtracked," Adam whispered to her. Adam stood and started toward the stranger, waving friendly, as he moved and the man closed the distance too, carrying a large pack with strange gear tied to its frame. "Howdy," Adam said. "How you doin'?"

"Who are you?" the man asked.

"Adam Shaw."

"Found anything yet?"

"I'm sorry?" Adam said.

"The girl. I know who you are. You're the one the locals call the Finder."

"I don't know you, sir. Help me out."

"My name is David. I work for the government. They flew me in."

"Flew you in?" Adam questioned.

"Yes. To find the bear."

"I see. Where you from?"

"Hell of a long way from here," the man said.

"So, you work for the Fish and Wildlife Service?" Adam asked.

"No. I'm under contract with another branch of the government. I research things."

"Like bears?"

"Grizzlies," David said.

"There are no grizzlies here," Adam said.

"You think not? Well, there shouldn't be," the man finished.

"How could that be?" Adam asked.

"When man's after money, nature is always changed. We've changed rivers, polluted oceans, cleared entire forests, all in the pursuit of money. Trust me, Mr. Shaw. If it were to make somebody rich, a grizzly here in the Smokies is no problem.

"Did a grizzly kill these people?" Adam asked seriously.

The man looked nervous, his eyes looking up before he answered. "The bear is close. You should be very careful. I don't want any others to be hurt by this bear. I would like to take the bear home before anything else happens to him."

"Home?" Micah asked. "Where's that?"

"It's not here," he said.

"You're concerned for the bear?" Micah asked.

The man smiled. "Seems strange to you that I care about this bear. I can understand that, but yes, I'm very concerned about this bear. What's happened is not his fault, you see."

"But he's killed people," she said.

The man looked wounded, staring at the ground. "I know. But he only does what nature tells him to do."

"The bear killed them. They're gone," she repeated.

"Do we hate tornadoes or floods or hurricanes that kill?" he said. "Not really. We fear them, curse our fate, but we don't blame them."

"Acts of God. Is that what you mean?" Micah asked.

"No," he said quickly. "God had no hand in this disaster, except ... " and he paused, " ... except in making us weak."

They stared at each other. "Why do you think he did that?" David said. "Wouldn't it have been better to make us strong?" the man continued.

Micah looked at Adam, amazed at the conversation, hoping for a hint of understanding from his face. "I don't think he made us weak," Adam said. "He made our decisions difficult."

"No sir. He made us weak. Very weak."

"I think," Adam said slowly, "that we learn from our mistakes."

"So you believe in redemption, Mr. Shaw?"

"Yes, I do. Do you?" Adam asked.

The stranger laughed loudly, with no hint of restraint. His laughter echoed off the trees around them. "I want to. But I can't seem to find it."

"Then find the bear," Adam said.

"I'll do my best." And he extended his hand to them and they shook it. "I am supposed to radio them if I see you, you know."

"Who?" Adam asked.

"There are many who want you off this mountain."

"Who?" Adam asked again.

"Forget 'em. They are not important," he said flatly. "Her name is Anna, I understand. Find her, Mr. Shaw. You do that for me. You find her."

"I'll do my best," Adam said.

"Anna," the stranger repeated and they noticed his face twisted with emotion. "Tell her that I am sorry. Tell her that I am very sorry."

Doc turned, walked away and then turned back to them. "Forget the guns," he said. "They aren't big enough. And he disappeared from them down the trail.

CHAPTER SEVENTEEN

*T*hey continued the track for two hours through the tangled mountain understory, the sun higher in its course, its heat spawning humidity that soaked their clothes with a sticky sweat and burned their eyes. Micah was tired, the intensity of the track through thick cover draining her energy. Adam stopped at the edge of a bluff that overlooked a vast timbered valley below. Nestled in the mountain range in the center of the valley was a timbered plateau that rose like some ancient burial mound that had been raised from the valley floor in homage to a distant sky. She stood beside him as they viewed the land and Micah felt some strange bond between them that she had not found before as if the sight itself, taken in by their eyes at this exact moment, somehow merged their spirits. He turned to her, as if feeling her thoughts.

"You're tired," he said.

"I'm okay."

"Let me have this," he said as he took her pack, lifting the weight of it from her shoulders and she slid from the straps. He rested the pack against a tree and removed his own and they sat in the leaves at the edge of the bluff, their backs against a huge basswood.

"It's called the Devil's Nest," he said, pointing with the shotgun toward the land below them.

"Why's that?" she asked.

"Who knows where a lot of these old names come from?" he said.

"You have to be sleepy. You didn't sleep last night, did you?" she asked.

"I'm fine," he said. "I'm worried about you, though."

"Don't worry about me," she said.

"I can't help it," he said.

Micah looked at him, but said nothing. The air was still. No breeze stirred. She flicked a piece of moss under her fingers, noticing the dirt on her hands. "That's the nicest thing you've ever said to me," she said. Then she shrugged and looked away.

"I didn't expect to like you so much. At first I wasn't sure," he said."

"Are you afraid of me?" she asked.

He didn't answer. "Are you afraid of *anything?*" she asked after a few moments.

"Yep," he said quickly.

"What?"

"High places and sharks."

She laughed. "Sharks?"

"Yeah. When I was a kid I used to swim all the time and sometimes the water would be dark. You know you couldn't see your feet when you tread water. I would sometimes think about a shark coming from deep below me and what it would feel like to see nothing and then have a shark at your feet."

"Well, you're in luck. There's no sharks down there," she smiled.

"You. What are you afraid of?" he asked.

"Anything that flies and stings," she answered. "Little ones or big ones, makes no difference."

"Actually it doesn't have to sting. If it looks like it could sting and is flying around me, I'm out of here."

"Well, I'll tell you, partner. You take care of the sharks and I'll swat the flying beasts."

"Deal," she said. She looked at him across their distance. His eyes were tired. "You have to sleep, Adam, even if it's just for a while. I did get *some* sleep last night. You haven't slept in days."

"She's down there, you know."

Micah looked at him but said nothing.

"Maybe you're right," he said. "She's close. Give me fifteen minutes. No more." He looked at his watch. He moved from his position and sat below her. "I'm gonna lean back against you," he said. "Hope you don't mind, but if the bear was to come, I have to know immediately without words."

She spread her legs immodestly allowing him to scoot backwards against her, his head at her breast level, the shotgun resting in his lap. "Lay your hands across my shoulders," he said. "Are you comfortable?"

"I'm fine," she whispered.

"If you see or hear anything, just tap me or whisper to the back of my head."

"Okay."

"And if I snore," he said, "poke me. Fifteen minutes, Micah. That's all."

"Sleep," she said. "Just sleep."

"Are you okay?" he asked.

"Shut your eyes," she ordered.

"You need to know something," he said.

"What?"

"I have no clue how to stop a grizzly bear except to keep shooting," he said.

"Go to sleep," she whispered.

Adam was asleep in thirty seconds. His head moved slowly to the left and relaxed. His breathing was deep and peaceful. Micah slowly moved her hands to the center of his chest and locked her fingers, and then gently rested her cheek against the top of his head. She briefly closed her eyes.

After a while, Adam dreamed.

They sat on his porch steps, he one step below her tucked between her knees, looking out over the vast wilderness in front of them. Her arms were around him and he rested his hands on hers as she whispered a long time in his ear. Occasionally, they would laugh, and only the birds would hear. Finally he turned and stood, then bent down and kissed her for a long time. He could smell her hair and he breathed it in like some potion that made him weak and delirious with her presence. She removed his shirt, never stopping the kisses and they laughed again as they fell backwards onto the porch.

He left the porch briefly and her lying there saying ... don't go — don't go ... but he returned from
inside the cabin with the bed's mattress and he
picked her up and placed her on it and she smiled as
he nestled against her, kissing her neck and her eyes
and her shoulders and lower between her breasts.
Her eyes were closed now and she arched her back
slightly ... and he kissed her again, gently brushing
her lips with his, then deeper, but still soft and she
moaned softly. He felt her fingers in his hair, pulling
him closer, and then on his back, her fingernails digging slightly while she moved beneath him. He wondered if she could feel his heart beating wildly
against her, her passion surrounding him like some
adoring cloud filled with her music that reached to
the center of him. She watched as he slowly
undressed her, gently kissing her body as he moved
down. Her head arched back again, exposing her
nakedness to the mountain air on that porch and
the birds sang around her in the dimness behind her
closed eyes, feeling him surround her, his hands
exploring her soft skin freely until she cried quietly
for him. He lost the feeling of time for his being
could not be filled with enough of her. Finally he collapsed beside her and closed his eyes, feeling her fingers gently caressing his face and her lips against his
mouth and her sweet breath he inhaled.

Adam was awakened by her gentle touch and the dream was gone like some painful separation of lovers' hearts for an instant, followed by a need to separate. He moved quickly from her touch and she looked at him with eyes that did not understand. "Adam, what's wrong?" Their eyes held each other for a long time and he reached down and touched her face and held her hair between his fingers.

"Nothing," and that was all he said before retrieving their gear. It took them another hour to make their way down the bluff to the hollow below. The temperature cooled, a fast-moving creek tumbling water over smooth rocks beside them as they walked, following Anna's tracks beneath the evergreens toward the Devil's Nest that loomed high above them in the distance.

Nearing the Devil's Nest, the canopy above them grew denser, blocking the sun's strength. A massive fallen trunk blocked their path and Adam could see that Anna had rolled beneath it, but they could not follow because of their packs, so they climbed the trunk and jumped to the other side. When they turned, the scene before them froze them in their tracks, causing their breathing to quicken and then slow as their eyes moved to take it in.

The sound came as quickly as the sight. Hundreds of thrushes and veeries appeared before them, all singing with fluted notes of ethereal power, rising and falling in their quivering melodies, like a feathered barrier of natural awe, so wonderful in its musical power. Adam turned to Micah and saw that she was smiling with pure pleasure, and he laughed to himself at the sound of this avian orchestra, its source dwarfing even thunderstorms and making the moonlight infantile in its art.

Then he looked down. The ground was torn for fifty yards in front of him, bear sign everywhere, scraping track marks, trees shredded with the bear's fury. He placed his hand on Micah's shoulder and from the look on his face, she lost her smile and they moved forward through the birds slowly, but the birdsong remained behind them, like some fence of sound to the outside.

There was a tree — a monster hemlock. It had partially fallen, its roots exposed at its base like twisted spears, and its length extended toward the bluff above it, hanging solitary over the creek that, at that point, fell fifty feet below in a cascading waterfall, so that there was great distance from the tree to the base of the falls. They moved slowly toward the tree, the ground around its roots torn, almost as if the tree itself was some shrine of activity. Their footfalls were silent since the ground was damp and the leaf mat soft, and Micah watched him peering ahead, his eyes constantly searching the space in front of them, his hands on the shotgun, like some bird hunter walking up a covey. Every few steps he would stop and quickly scan the ground at their feet and then his eyes would jerk up, as a deer would act while feeding. There was no sound, save the water in the creek, and they both noticed the silence of the birds at the same time, and they looked behind them, but the birds were not visible.

"Look," he said, pointing with his boot to a print in the soil. It was a massive track, some ten inches across and Micah tried to imagine the paw that made that sign and the leg attached to a body so immense and she remembered the sound it had made in the night that seemed to rattle the trees and shake her soul with its source. They moved on slowly.

At the base of the tree there was dried blood on the ground, and blood stained the twisted roots and there was hair on the roots and signs of great struggle. Some of the roots had been broken and chewed and there were signs of digging in the soil that had remained with the roots "I don't understand this," he said. He looked back at Micah whose eyes were staring up into the tree, transfixed on something far away, hanging over the open space above the falls.

"Look," she whispered.

The Finder's eyes saw. Anna was there, at the top of the tree, her arms outstretched holding two limbs, sitting on the trunk.

"Would you please get the binoculars from my pack?" he asked her in a matter-of-fact tone, and turned his back to her. Adam handed her the shotgun and focused the lenses on Anna. "She's alive," he whispered. "Her eyes are closed. Micah, can you imagine what she's been through? Okay. We have to get her down. She's probably too weak to move, so this is gonna be tricky and we have a *big* problem."

"I know," she said. "There's sharks in that tree."

Adam turned to her and smiled. "We found her, partner. She's *alive*." He pulled Micah close and Micah forgot about the bear for that time and she felt his happiness in this wilderness place where so much violence lived and strangely the fear of dying left her, the finding of Anna alive overpowering it and the strength she felt in Adam, her new partner, bonding it with something she had never felt before. "Should you call to her?" she asked.

"I don't think she can hear," he said while removing ropes from his pack.

"Why not?"

"She's not here," he said. "She's removed herself from here."

"Let me do it," she offered.

"Why?"

"I climb," she said. "Heights don't bother me."

"What if she can't walk? Can you carry her back?"

"Can you?" she asked.

"I don't know." Adam admitted.

"Let's both go."

He thought about that. "Okay," he agreed.

With a small rope he tied their packs and the shotgun together and hoisted them over a nearby limb, pulling them high in case the bear returned. Then he tied a longer rope to a large root and tested it with his weight and then they squeezed between the tangle of roots using them as steppingstones to get above the rootball and onto the trunk. "You go first," he said.

"Why am I tied off?" Micah asked. "You're the one who'll probably fall."

"I only have one long rope," he said. "We'll tie Anna off when we get there."

They scooted forward toward Anna, hanging over the moist air of the falls, working their way between limbs that scratched their arms and faces, but at least gave some sense of security, something to hang on to. Adam looked ahead, never down. He watched as Micah maneuvered between the branches, carefully placing each hand, each move forward a planned action and he followed her. Five more feet and he stopped.

"Talk to me," he said to her back.

"No. Concentrate," she said moving ahead.

"I am. I'm concentrating on the ability of my body to shut down. I can't move."

Micah turned her head. She was some thirty feet out and Adam was ten feet behind her. His color had paled and his hands were frozen to two limbs on either side of the trunk. "Adam," she said sternly. "You can do this. It's a cakewalk."

He tried to smile. "My mind is fine. My body won't work right."

"Make it work right! Adam Shaw! You get your ass up here! I didn't go all this way to end up alone."

Adam looked through the limbs between them and found Micah's eyes, urging him to find a strength that had eluded him since a child. He breathed a deep breath of mountain air and looked at Anna. Her eyes were now open and her arms extended toward him and as Adam watched, the young girl attempted to stand, wobbly kneed and unsure. "No!" Adam yelled.

Micah turned to see Anna standing, smiling at Adam, and when Micah looked back at Adam, he was standing on that massive tree and walking toward her, surefooted and strong. Stepping around her he said, "go back" touching her shoulder and continued on. "Anna," he said when reaching her, "I've come to take you home."

Anna was weeping when Adam reached across their space and held her, holding her close to him, weakened and frail, her hair tangled and matted, dried blood on her face and her clothes, her skin scratched and torn. He felt her go limp in his arms and he held her up and then lifted the young girl and turned to see Micah behind him, breaking limbs to clear his return path. Her hands were bleeding from her work. "I'll never leave you alone," she said. "Don't ever tell me to leave you again."

Anna opened her eyes, looking at Micah, and smiled faintly. "I was afraid you wouldn't come," she whispered and then closed her eyes again.

They made her a bed at the base of that fallen hemlock and gave her water and food. Adam stood guard, shotgun in hand, with his back to them while Micah bathed her with water from the creek and he could hear Micah's gentle voice reassuring her and when he turned Anna had fallen asleep wearing clean clothes that Micah had produced from her pack. "I had to cut her hair," Micah whispered.

They stood together watching Anna sleep. "I found blood in her tracks, not much, but a drop every now and again. Is she menstruating?" he asked.

"Yes," Micah nodded.

"I see," he said. "Can you help her?"

"Of course. Bless her heart. She used her socks."

"It's real important to get rid of that scent. Where are her clothes?"

"They should be a mile downstream by now," she said.

Adam put his arm around Micah's shoulder. "Good. I want you to get some sleep, okay?"

"I don't know if I can."

"Take my bag. Put it next to her. Hold her hand. Forget everything else."

"When can we leave?"

"It depends on Anna, but not before tomorrow morning. I want to get some more food in her and … "

"What?" she asked.

Adam stared at the ground to his left. The tracks were plain. Lots of them. And he had not seen them before they went after Anna in the tree. Unshod horse tracks. "Nothing," he said. "Get some sleep, okay?"

GARY COOK

CHAPTER EIGHTEEN

*H*e sat cross-legged, watching them sleep in
the glow of the fire, the burning wood
popping like tiny firecrackers, sending orange
sparkles skyward. Micah held Anna's hand and
Adam mused at the sight, the steel barrel of the
shotgun cool against his cheek, a support for his
head. Anna's fingers were long and delicate;
Micah's shorter but strong. Sleeping, they were at
peace joined together like that, two hands that
had never touched, two souls bound in some cir-
cumstance of fate or chance, he could not be
sure, but bound nevertheless into some state-
ment of the future of which he was a part.

The fire popped again, louder this time and Micah opened her eyes. She focused on Adam and then the fire and then back to the man across from her. "How long have I slept?" she asked.

"Five hours, I guess. Go back to sleep. Everything's fine."

She saw that he had prepared a supper and the food was heating against the coals. "I had a dream about you," she said. "We were drinking muscadine wine and I was telling you this great theory of mine about the Melungeons. It made you laugh."

Adam smiled. "What theory is that?"

"Will you laugh?"

"I hope so," he said.

She sat upright and combed the hair from her face with her fingers. "Okay. Here goes. I never told you this before. My theory is that if the Melungeons were the lost tribe of Israel, and possibly they took with them the Ark of the Covenant and the Ark is somewhere hidden in the Appalachian Mountains."

He looked at her in the firelight.

"It's not that crazy, really. Look, the Ark was moved by priests in 200 B.C. because idolatry was being practiced in the same temple where the Ark was kept. They took it to some island in Egypt, but mysteriously the people who guarded it disappeared, as well as the Ark. What if those Jews who disappeared are the descendants of the Melungeons? What better way to protect the location of the Ark than to leave it with a people who have no clue as to their origin? Well?" she asked.

"Maybe it is," he said," but it might be better to understand the truth of a theory, and not get hung up on the theory itself."

"And what is the truth of that theory?" she asked.

"What is the Ark?" he asked. "It holds the proof of God's contact with His people. Micah, look at what's happened here. The proof is right in front of you. I'd say you found your Ark."

She thought silently staring into the flames of the fire, and then looked up at him. "The Melungeon girl. What is her role in all this?" she said. She tossed a twig into the coals.

"Maybe she brought you here," he said.

A barred owl called behind them. "Being afraid to leave you brought me here."

He stood, walked across the firelight, knelt and repositioned some logs on the fire. "If you would quit fighting the obvious, I think you would see clearer," he said.

"It's obvious to me we aren't on the same

page," she said.

"You want the same page?"

"Yes, I do," she said.

"I dreamed about you when I slept this morning," he said. She said nothing, afraid to. "We were together, living at my house," he continued. *"Now, how does that help us? To talk about that?"* he asked.

"It helps me," she said. "It lets me know we start from the same place, even if you don't allow yourself to stay there. I am screwed up. Totally confused. I can't make this quantum leap into your world so quickly, so help me make the transition. Just talk to me. Show me where you started."

He paused, staring into the fire. "I'll try," he said finally.

Micah searched for something appropriate to say, but her thoughts were jumbled, falling over themselves in her consciousness.

"Have you ever been married?" she asked finally

"No, never figured it could work."

"What do you mean?"

He stood. "The only peace I've ever known is here." Raising his arms, he gestured to the woods around him. "My family. The only family I have ever really known is here." He paused. "What about you?" he asked.

"What?"

"Been married?"

"Yes. Once. Lasted seven years or one year, depending on how you look at it," she said.

"What happened?" he asked.

"It just wasn't right. You know it's supposed to be wonderful. It wasn't."

"Why? Why wasn't it wonderful?" he asked.

"I think that it's impossible for me to be happy without becoming vulnerable. You know, to talk about anything that you wonder about or dream about. If two people can't talk, honestly talk, it seems hopeless."

"I always wondered what it would be like to have a family, you know in those times when you just let your mind wander," he said. He looked up at Micah. "I think I finally have a hint of that, here with you and Anna. I want to thank you for that."

"I think I've looked for you my whole life," she said. "Since I was a little girl."

Anna jerked and was awake, frantically reaching out for limbs to steady her on the tree and Adam caught one arm and Micah the other until her breathing slowed and she looked at them, back and forth. "It's all right. It's all right," Adam whispered.

Anna looked at him. "You came," she said. "You came."

"Took me a while," he smiled. "You kinda wandered around a bit."

"At first, I thought you were Zeke, our guide, but he was killed and then I thought I was alone, that you were dead, but you came."

"And I'm gonna take you home. But first, we have to make you strong again. Are you hungry?" he asked.

"I'm starving," she said.

"Good," he said. "Let me get you a proper supper."

"Wait!" she said. "What is your name, and yours?" she asked turning to Micah.

"I'm Adam."

"Micah," she said smiling.

"Adam ... Micah," she repeated.

Anna ate her supper without talking and took the food slowly like Adam had told her. Adam was reluctant to question her about the bear or the attacks in fear that the memories would be too troubling for her. "The night was the worst," she said finally. "Particularly with the moon."

"The moon?" Micah asked.

"Yes. The last two nights," she said staring into

the fire with no emotion.

"It's red," Adam said. They looked around in the sky but it had not yet risen.

"In the end, the moon shall turn to blood," she continued.

"The end of what?" Micah asked.

"I don't know," she said. "The end of something, though — the last week, month, year, century, we can't know. Time is unimportant, except as it relates to our own lives."

"And where did that come from, about the moon turning to blood," Micah asked.

"The books of Joel, Acts, several places," she said into the fire. "Many religions." And the fire popped again sending sparks swirling upward, but Anna did not blink.

"Anna," Micah said, "what does that mean to you?"

Anna turned to Micah. "It means that things are different now, that some people will be able to know things that others don't. It means that two worlds will merge during this time and reality will include a spiritual plane that before could not be seen, but can be seen now."

"How could you know that?" Micah asked. "How could you possibly know that?"

Anna stood and went to Adam laying her

hand upon his shoulder. "And how could I know that this man sees things that others can't and he has never told another living soul, except you."

Adam looked at Micah, "Do you understand now?" he asked.

"No," Micah said.

"What do you know *for sure?*" he asked Micah.

"I know I care about you and because you wanted to find Anna so badly, I care about her too. That's all I know."

"And you, Anna? What do you know for sure?" he asked.

"That I'm glad you're here, both of you," Anna said.

"There you have it," he said. "For right now that is all we need to know."

In the glow of that fire the night birds comforted them, and they didn't fear the bear again until the screaming started on the path they had followed to the tree. Anna jerked her head to see Micah watching Adam whose eyes were staring toward the direction of the horrible sounds in the night. The screaming suddenly stopped.

"He came to the tree before you this morning, a man with some sort of radio receiver or something. He never saw me in the tree. Then he went off like he was following something," Anna said.

"I tried to call to him, but he didn't hear me."

"I didn't see his tracks," Adam said.

"He came from that way," Anna pointed. "Not the way you came."

"Anna, the man who came to the tree … he said to tell you that he was sorry," Adam said.

"I know," she said. "He kept saying it as he walked."

"He was tracking the bear," he said.

"How?" Micah asked.

"A transmitter," Adam said.

"When did the bear get a transmitter?" she asked.

Adam picked up the shotgun.

"The beast won't come here," Anna said. "He came the first night and tried all night to get into the tree. He is mad, you know, biting the air and screaming. The second night he came back. The birds sing when he comes and I sang too, the song they taught me. It was dark, but I saw a man riding a red horse and he stood over there in the pines and behind him were red horses, speckled, and white. The beast stopped when they came and screamed at them, but they wouldn't leave me."

"Men on horses?" Micah asked.

"I saw the one before. He has a big scar on his face. I could see it in the moonlight, but he has nice eyes," Anna said.

"Was there an Indian, with long hair," Micah asked.

"I'm not sure," she said.

"It wouldn't be him," Adam said.

"Why not?" Micah asked.

"He said he couldn't protect me from the bear?"

"He said he couldn't protect you from the bear. Maybe he could protect Anna. Don't even think about going out there," Micah told Adam.

"Do you know these riders?" he asked Anna.

"I know the book of Zechariah. I have seen the big one with the scar. He was there after my parents were killed."

"In Africa?" Micah asked.

"Yes. These riders are of God. They aren't men. That's the truth, but if you wish they can be ordinary men on horses. It's your choice."

They were quiet for a time and the fire talked, the warmth of it touching their faces. "All this mysticism, things you seem to understand that I don't. Life is not like this, at least for me," Micah said.

"Life *is* like this," Adam said. "Since the beginning of man, life has been like this. We've prayed to the heavens, begged for mercy, love, help, understanding. Nothing has been more central to our civilizations than belief in a greater power. The question is, Micah, has man really believed or has it been one big fairy tale to ease our emptiness?"

"You mean is God a Santa Claus?" Micah asked.

"That is one of the two questions. Pure and simple," Anna said.

They looked at her. "All this is real," Anna whispered, "as real as the trees, as real as our hearts."

"I don't want to deal with this great mystery of life," Micah said. "Am I so bad for that? I want to be happy. I want to live happily ever after. I want to make you laugh, Adam. I want to lie on a beach in the Bahamas and drink rum. I think God wants us to be happy ... doesn't He?"

"Yes," Anna said, "but everyday life is a great distraction for the soul. We can't be truly happy unless we face these questions. We can't avoid it. We can't put it off forever. You will confront these questions. We all will."

"You asked one of the questions," Micah said. "What's the other?"

Anna looked at her. "Why were you born?"

CHAPTER NINETEEN

*T*he bear had not slept since its escape. The worm's movement behind its eyes made sleep impossible, a torment it could not understand, the instinct to sleep so strong, and so its madness continued. Without sleep the bear found satisfaction only in feeding, for after gratifying its hunger there was a brief rest from the suffering and a feeling that sleep might come. The bear shut its little eyes, its wet chin resting on the bloodied, dismembered torso of the two-legged it had found sleeping on the trail.

It had no memory of this two-legged, no unique scent that linked it to the man who had plucked him from his winter sleep so far away. There was no hatred, no malice, no thought of revenge ... just the violent action that kept it alive. It had no pity for itself about the growing worm in its brain, no thought of death, the concept of nonexistence was an impossibility. It lived, driven by instincts of a thousand years that had been placed in its blood by the same maker of the stars. There was nothing in its world except life. There was only life, and the pain or contentment offered by instinct, driven by some higher force it could not understand.

*   *   *

Adam Shaw tried to understand his life. He could not sleep, lying awake beside the girls who slept quietly, their fingers touching lightly in the fire's glow. He pondered his existence, the possibility of his death, love, compassion, duty, devotion to those who loved him, happiness, laughter, and why he was born. Now was his chance to finish it. He felt comfortable in leaving them around the fire, the light that offered protection from the blackness. He believed Anna's earlier words about the safety of the ground beneath them. From somewhere deep he knew the inevitable concerning the bear.

The realization of the recurring dream he had experienced for six months was near, the power of the charge, the terror of its power. He sighed. It was better to do it now, away from them. The bear was close and maybe sleeping after the kill. The darkness bothered him, but if he was careful and very patient the chances of his survival were somewhat better. Even if he didn't survive, he had acquired a great respect for Micah's ability to get Anna back to civilization, provided the bear was killed. Adam moved quietly to his pack and removed a pair of thick wool socks that he pulled over his boots to soften his footfalls. He then wrote Micah a note.

Micah,

I leave you my compass and the shotgun. Walk 45 degrees to a logging road and follow it east to a highway. It should take one day. I know you can do this. You are very brave. It is all that counts. Everything else follows the heart. History is yours.

Adam

He left the note between them and moved back to the fire. He removed the revolver from his holster and checked the rounds. He remembered loading them at the upper limits for a .44 Magnum and carefully molding the bullets, mixing them extremely hard for needed penetration. Turning one round over in the firelight, he studied its form and returned it to its black hole, quietly closing the cylinder. Adam looked in the direction of the earlier screaming, beyond the firelight, into the darkness of the mountain. He bowed his head, pausing for a long time and then disappeared into the blackness to find the color of Doc's trail.

Away from the firelight he waited twenty minutes to allow his eyes time to adjust. The moon cast an eerie hue into the woods in front of him but he was thankful for the light it provided. He would go very slowly, allowing all of his senses to guide him. One step. Wait one minute. One step. Wait one minute. Sometimes he would wait five minutes or ten, he couldn't be sure. Watching. Smelling. Feeling the woods around him. After three hours he was close. There was a clearing of sorts in front of him, a space without trees. He stopped, crouching behind a trunk, his right hand touching the bark. He waited. Nothing moved in front of him for a long time, and then it did.

Like some arm of darkness, a shadow moved, rising briefly and then down again. He thought it moved. Maybe not. He waited, peering beside the shadow, not directly at it, for his peripheral vision was better. He waited — patient. His nose gave the first clue, a soured smell, brief, but real, that touched the center of his brain and was gone. He strained to see the black form again, a hint as to the movement's source. He closed his eyes, breathing slowly, trying to feel the presence before him. He could feel the night around him, its blackness cloaking him like some sheer garment that protected not, and it was then that he felt *behind* him the center of his fear. He heard a breath, an exhaling of the night's air, black and foul smelling and a padded breaking of a twig beneath some weight that powered that breath … and with a calmness, Adam turned.

For an instant he saw nothing, but then a great shadow rose, its form comprehensible to him, and he raised the gun, its black sights useless against the dark form that towered above him, and, as he pressed the trigger, the night exploded with sound from the form, a roar so intense that Adam winced in pain and the gun discharged, the muzzle blast blinding him, but not before he saw the sights in the fire before him, the front sight off considerably to the right and the bear frozen, standing like some monument to power. The roar changed to a scream and Adam felt the blow to his chest knocking him backwards and he fired twice more while falling. He rolled after feeling the ground beneath him and was on his feet again, but tripped quickly and fell again.

Adam froze, feeling the thing beneath his hand, cold and without life but so humanly familiar. The face under his living fingers stared open-eyed into the night, wet with sticky blood and without spirit to move or object. He moved his hand quickly away, staring face to face with the dead man in the dimness. The bear moved closer, walking toward him, the frothing breath bubbling louder as it neared until the beast stood over him looking down into the living face of Adam Shaw who remained still, like the dead man beside him until in one fluid motion, Adam raised the pistol and touched the bear's underside pulling the trigger three times, and the blast and recoil forced his wrist backwards and there was a great pressure on his chest and his ears heard ringing and his head was jerked sideways, his arm twisted quickly behind him.

There was a great crashing in the brush beside him and he heard the roar of pain and more crashing and breaking of limbs and then it was silent. Adam lay still trying to breathe, but his chest was broken somehow and the pain was terrible. His arm was lying awkwardly behind him and with his right hand he pulled the useless limb back around to its normal position. When he tried to stand his head throbbed with such force that he lost his balance and fell, tasting the leafy dirt under his face.

*   *   *

The shots startled Micah from her sleep and she rose in a panic, looking all around for Adam, and then she heard the roar and Anna stood beside her. "Adam!" she yelled, and she ran for the shotgun and started into the darkness.

"No," said Anna. "Wait."

"For what?" she yelled.

"For me. Listen."

"To what?" Micah asked.

"Shush. Please," Anna said.

They stood there in the glow of that fire, Micah's chest rising and falling with each breath and Anna with her head bowed listening for something. Anything. And they both heard it at the same time. A thrush called and then again, getting closer. "What is that?"

"It's him," Anna said.

"No," Micah said.

"He's coming," Anna whispered.

Micah saw Adam's note and picked it up, reading while they waited and then stared into the darkness, waiting, waiting, waiting until finally they heard limbs breaking beyond the fire's light. Micah stood beside Anna with the shotgun leveled in the direction of the sounds when they heard his voice. "Micah. Put the gun down."

She ran to his voice and so did Anna and from the darkness they emerged with the Finder, one on each side of him helping him walk. He was soaked in blood and they eased him down beside the fire, his back against a fallen trunk. Micah began washing his face and the blood from his arms and chest and he said nothing for a long time and finally he raised his eyes toward Anna. "I messed up," he whispered. "I'm sorry," and then to Micah, "Hey honey, I'm home."

Both held him close, his blood staining their clothes and painting their skin. "You're alive," Micah whispered.

He looked at her and tried to smile but winced in pain. "You make me smile," he said.

"Where are you hurt?" she asked.

"Heck, just pick a place," he said. "Here, here, here, and here," he pointed with his good hand. "Ribs are broken and so's my collar-bone. My head feels like it's gonna explode."

"Here, I'll make a sling." She removed her scarf and tied it to hold his arm; then she retrieved a towel from her pack and wrapped his torso and his chest which glistened with blood and sweat in the firelight.

"The bear? "Micah asked.

"He's shot. Probably not dead yet, but he'll die. Maybe he's dead now. I hope so," he said.

When she finished he was delirious, mumbling incoherently while holding his head, and then his words were understandable. He was singing and the girls looked at each other in amazement. The tune was clear; his words slurred. "Prayfortheforest praytothetree prayfor thefishinthedeepbluesea. Prayforyourself andfor God'ssakeprayforme. Poor wretched unbeliever."

"James Taylor," Micah smiled. "He's half-dead and singing James Taylor."

"He's mad at himself," Anna said.

"What?"

"We make decisions that we think are right and when they don't work out the way we thought, we blame ourselves."

"Honey, you don't know the half of it," Micah said. "He did it for you."

"He's here for you," Anna said. "And you don't know the half of it."

Micah looked at her. "Then tell me."

Anna took his hand while she talked and quickly he was asleep. "His whole life he's wanted to know what it's like to be like everyone else — wife ... children ... to give himself to them. For life to be so simple as to work hard and love and laugh and sleep and do it all again the next day."

"How do you know what he feels?"

"Because I'm the same. I'll never have those things and it hurts. And in my dreams I have known him since I was very young."

"In your dreams?"

"Yes. Have you ever had a dream with the same person in it over and over, but you don't know the person?"

"No, I haven't."

"Well, I have. And I've been looking for this man for a long time," Anna said. "And so have you."

"And you think God is behind those dreams. God is talking to you," Micah said.

Anna looked up at the wounded moon, coursing blood-like across the mountain sky. "It's a special time, when God will pour out his spirit upon all flesh, and sons and daughters will prophesy and young men will see visions," Anna said. "You are a prophet."

"A daughter," Anna said. "I am a daughter, like you."

"Me?"

"Your father's name was Philip, with one L. So was mine."

Micah just looked at her. "You're wrong," Micah said. "I'm no prophet and God doesn't talk to me. I wish he did, but it doesn't happen."

Anna smiled and looked at Adam. "You love him?"

"Yes," Micah said.

"You feel connected to him?"

"Like I never thought possible," Micah said.

"Do you honestly think our Father speaks to us in words?" Anna asked.

They looked up to see Adam awake and staring at them. "Come here," he said. "Both of you." They moved closer and with his good hand he pulled Micah to him. "Anna, come on this side." With his good hand he moved his bad arm and held it high so that she could slip under it and she did. And he leaned back against the tree, Micah and Anna under each arm and he sighed. "Now," he said, "I am a happy man. Let's count stars or something." He paused and they could tell his voice trembled just a bit when he spoke. "Life is good and worth fighting for, and … I love you both very much. Very much."

"We love you too," Micah said.

CHAPTER TWENTY

*A*t first light there was a white smoke rising from the coals of the fire and the dew covered the land with a dampness that chilled the air. Anna was asleep in Adam's lap and Micah curled in a fleece blanket against him. He was stiff and sore, afraid to move fearing the pain that might come. His head was clear though and not throbbing and he was thankful for that. In that period of time between first light and the sun actually showing itself he pondered the bear, reliving the fight, trying to remember the bullet placement, knowing the bear was gut shot with the last round, knowing the bear was shot somewhere in the chest during the first volley. It had been five or six hours. Long enough for the bear to die. Maybe.

He felt Micah move against him and then she slowly raised her head. "Mornin'," she said.

"Hey," he smiled.

"How you feel?"

"Stiff," he said.

"Can you walk?"

"I'll have to. We're going home today," he said.

"Home," Micah whispered. "I forgot where that might be."

"C'mon," he said. "Let's get her up and me straightened out."

Later, when they were packed and ready to move out, Adam turned to see Anna alone at the base of the leaning tree looking up into its limbs. She touched its twisted roots, and turned as if leaving a dear friend for the last time. "My tree house," she said.

They left that place in the cool of the morning following Adam's direction. He moved slowly and his face showed pain when he walked, but there was an easiness in his manner that Micah noticed. He checked his pistol, making sure it was loaded, holstered it, and carried only the compass in his hand. They headed northeast from the Devil's Nest. By traveling northeast, they would cross an old logging trail after five miles and then walk it to Highway 226. From there safety was almost assured, for help should be waiting and it would be over. He was almost out of the mountains, almost successful in the job he promised God, almost able to rest.

The northeast course took them up a grade and the climb was slow and difficult in places, but it was the shortest route to safety and away from the last sighting of the bear. After two hours they had crested the mountain, resting at a rock outcrop that provided a panoramic view of Appalachia, with fog rising from the lowlands, and a feeling of loneliness within the green of the Pisgah National Forest.

"If my map's right, we'll be out by dark," he said. "I know it's slow going, but in the long run, it's the quickest."

"How are you?" Micah asked.

"I'm fine," he said.

Micah dug in her pack. "Anna, you're awfully quiet," he said. "What ya thinkin' so deep?"

"Isn't it strange how pain teaches," she said.

Micah handed Adam some aspirin. "Here, take these." He took them and drank from his canteen.

"It's not dead," Anna said.

Adam stopped drinking and looked at her.

"I know." He finished the drink. "Like you said, easy times never taught us much." He winked at her. In two minutes they were moving down the mountain through huge trunks of brown and a green canopy roof that almost blocked the blue sky.

After two hours of walking, he suddenly announced to them, "I refuse to be anything but happy today." Micah looked at him, bewildered. "C'mon," he said. "Smile. Where could you be having more fun than this?"

Micah laughed, softly at first and then louder until she grabbed a tree to hold herself up and they gathered around her, laughing with her, their voices echoing in the forest and the laughter caused Adam to wince in pain but he could not stop and Anna sat in the leaves and covered her mouth because she suddenly had the hiccups and that made them laugh harder. When they had finished and stood teary-eyed together in the silence of the forest, they embraced at the tree where Anna stood and they stood there for a long time holding each other tightly.

That was when it came, loping like some furred demon, its form moving through the trees with a limp, dragging behind it twenty feet of its own intestines, matted with leaves and dirt and blood. It gave a low growl as it ran down the hill toward them, popping its teeth and slinging its head from right to left, frothing at the mouth with bubbles of crimson blood. They stood there watching it come, Micah feeling Adam's hand pushing her behind him and somewhere she heard him say, "Take Anna and run," and she grabbed Anna and held her tightly, but did not run and they watched as Adam moved away from them toward the great bear.

As the bear neared Adam, he drew his pistol and fired, striking the bear with each round, knocking it to its knees at first, but it was up again and down, and up once again rising in its full length and with the last round Adam crammed the barrel under the bear's chin and pulled the trigger as the bear swung its great arms together and Adam was caught by its last strength as the bear fell. It rolled with Adam in its embrace, then convulsed in great spasms of death, coughed blood in its final breath and died.

Adam lay still with his back resting against the bear's belly, his head slumped down when Micah reached him. Anna was in tears, taking his hand and kneeling at his side. Micah lifted his face.

His eyes were open.

"Adam!" she yelled. He blinked and tried to focus on her face. His breaths were very weak. "Oh, Adam," Micah said.

"It's not his fault," he whispered.

"Don't be afraid," Anna said forcing a smile. "We'll take care of you."

Blood formed in Adam's mouth and Micah blotted it with her sleeve. "Adam. Look at me, Adam. You're going to be fine."

He smiled and with his good hand slowly touched her face. He spoke slowly, struggling with the words. "There is only one love. We show ... each other." The Finder winced in pain and then relaxed. "Anna," he struggled to look at her, "don't you cry, I'll be fine."

Adam Shaw looked through the canopy of the green wilderness to the blue sky. "It is a fine day," he whispered. "I refuse to be anything ... but ... happy."

Anna smiled, and while holding the Finder's hand next to her cheek, she whispered a prayer with tight-closed eyes. Adam turned, smiled briefly at her, and then breathed no more. Afterwards, they would not leave him, Micah holding his hand and Anna silently praying at his side.

They were faint at first, but the footsteps grew louder above them in the trees. Looking up they saw seven horses with riders, huge horses that were magnificent in their spirit, and the riders with sad faces dismounted and walked behind them and Micah saw Jack, and his face showed great emotion. Two of the larger riders held Anna's hands and another placed his hands on Micah's shoulders and they stood there for a long time in the silence of that green mountain of the Appalachian forest.

The largest rider, the one who held Anna's hand, had a severe scar that ran across his face, but his eyes were of the gentlest nature, and he spoke. "We will show you the way. Leave him. We will take him home. Don't be afraid."

Micah looked at this rider as she stood facing him. "I won't leave him."

"You must. He is not here."

Her face twisted as she cried. "I don't understand," she said.

"Yes, you do. It is difficult to believe a truth that is unseen. But you have seen. With your own eyes."

She looked back at Adam and Jack was kneeling beside him and he gently placed his hand on Adam's face, closing his eyes. "You said you couldn't protect him from the bear. I want to know why," Micah asked.

Jack stood. "I could not."

"But you could have stopped the bear and none of this would have happened."

"See that his death here is not his end, you will understand. It was his choice to die for you. *I would not take that from him.* You walked with him. Do you believe your life is important? He did."

Micah kneeled, touching Adam's face and said nothing more. After a while she stood and took Anna's hand.

GARY COOK

CHAPTER TWENTY-ONE

*M*icah stood in the front yard staring at Adam's house, already it seemed lonely without his presence, his attention, his spirit. The dog came trotting from behind the house in a wide circle, avoiding her as he moved, never barking but intent on a direction to get around her toward the long driveway and the county road below.

Upon seeing the dog she immediately cried, wanting to touch him, hold him in her arms, wanting the dog to take refuge in her compassion so that together, man and beast, they could find some spirit of understanding, some kinship

214

of loss and gain. She called his name. He stopped, looking toward her, and after a while turned his head toward the wildness of the deep timber and then back to Micah. The dog trotted toward the trees, his eyes holding on her while steadfastly moving away until finally turning, the Finder's dog was gone from her sight.

Micah stood perfectly still as if paralyzed by some human force of weak indecision, knowing not whether to strike out and find History or let him go, finding her own course away from him. She stood there for a long time, the pain in her chest so intense that she briefly contemplated the possibility of her heart stopping and that she might die before making her decision.

Finally, she dropped to her knees and collapsed looking up into a blue sky, the same blue as the Melungeon porch painted with faith to bar evil spirits. She felt the cool grass beneath her and heard a breeze in the leaves behind her. She closed her eyes, exhausted. The pain in her heart was so deep, so devastating, that she wished to die. Just die ...

She felt his breath first and smelled him next and she opened her eyes to see the dog looking down into her face. "You came back," she whispered through wet eyes. History whined and slowly lowered his head to her hand and licked it once and then again like tending some wound that needed attention. She moved her hands to his neck and pulled him closer and the dog rested his head on her breast and she held that dog against her as she sobbed, feeling his compassion, his desire to be loved, like all things under God's blue sky.

After a while, she prayed. Unlike any prayer in her life, it was without words, an opening of her heart to the sky above her without restraint … just a mournful soul lying in the grass with a dog at her breast and the silent presence of a man who could see colors when others could not. History was hers. She had been brave and for the first time, after lying there for hours, openhearted to the sky, she began to understand about love and the search for truth. Adam had been right, maybe there is but one true love and we are all guides to each other in finding it. The loves we find here on Earth, are only glimpses of its larger perfection, its complete compassion … its marvelous color.

EPILOGUE

We had been waiting at Highway 226 when Micah and Anna arrived, just like the Finder had asked. They walked out alone and for some reason did not act surprised that we were waiting. Two wildlife officers took Anna to her grandfather, but Micah refused to leave and she took us back to the site where the Finder had died.

When we arrived, his body was gone. We searched the rest of the day and the next, but could not find him. We arranged for the bear to be transported to the Center for Wildlife Diseases in Atlanta where a full necropsy was performed the next week. The animal's brain was heavily infested with a brain worm commonly carried by raccoons. It can only be surmised what effect the parasite had on the mental capacity of the bear. We did, however, find the partial remains of a Dr. David Johnson who had obviously been killed by the bear. There were rumors about a trio of locals who got drunk and went hunting the bear several days before, but we found no traces of those boys.

At noon the following day, the townspeople of Sneedville in Hancock County were amazed to see a magnificent white horse walk through the center of their town. The horse pulled a travois, its wooden ends resonating against the pavement, carrying the body of Adam Shaw under a colorful blanket. A large crowd gathered and followed behind the horse. There was complete quiet as they walked except for the sound of the wooden travois poles against the concrete and the horse's unshod hooves as he walked. The horse stopped at the courthouse square and when Doc Green removed the blanket the onlookers saw Adam Shaw neatly dressed in a flannel shirt and jeans.

We could find no family to notify. His only family was a dozen wildlife officers and hundreds of friends that he had touched in some way over the years. The entire Melungeon community was present and of course there was Micah and Anna, who

Gary Cook

attended the funeral with Anna's grandfather. The Finder was buried behind his house on a hill that overlooked a vast section of the mountain. At the end of the service Anna sang a song. It was haunting. No one would speak or move after she finished. I remember a red-tailed hawk screamed in the sky above us. I also remember that Micah and Anna talked after the ceremony and in the end they prayed together at the gravesite and then held each other for a long time and they both cried when Anna left. The Melungeons gathered around them in the end and laid their hands on them.

I was one of those wildlife officers who considered him a brother. None of us objected to Micah moving into the house with History. As a matter of fact, we liked the idea. I saw Micah again at his house a week after the funeral. We sat on the porch and drank lemonade and she was very timid at first, shy almost in talking about Adam. She said quietly that she had loved him very much and then became teary and she would hug the dog and remain quiet for a long time. I talked about my life in those periods of her silence, my love of the land, my family. I told game warden stories that made her laugh and she would always ask what Adam did and then say, "No don't tell me. Let me guess," and she always did.

I stopped often to check on her. We all did. In the

219

winter she was writing and when we talked she would cry because she said it wasn't right. She said that for some reason her words weren't good enough to capture what had happened, the emotion of her time with him. I asked to read it, but she refused. She cried all winter and sat staring at the fire, holding the dog. There were rumors that she was seen at night making trips deep into the mountains to see the Melungeon girl and that the girl would only speak to Micah and no one else.

In the spring, she stopped crying. I came upon her one day in the yard staring deeply into the underbrush beside the house.

"Listen," she said. "It's a thrush."

She smiled, and then she smiled bigger, like some answer had just been delivered and I was supposed to know, but I didn't.

"What?" I asked.

"Adam always said to live for the next five minutes. I have been living in the past. You," she said, "You can do it right. I've read your words. You write from the heart."

"I write short stories," I said.

"Listen to me," she said. "I won't make you guess like they did to me, but don't be afraid. We all work together. I affect you when I care about you and you someone else and so on and so on. See?"

I just looked at her.

"When you think you know what it is you should do, you find out that maybe you can't do it. Adam thought I could write this. He thought that was my purpose. And now, I can't. I'm sorry. I just can't get it right. But because he died, I met you and we became friends. Be my brother. Be my friend. Let me tell you everything. I can tell it, but I can't write it. Please. Please do it for Adam … and me. We are all connected."

"I wish you would just talk plainly," I said. "Your words confuse me."

"I'm sorry. I'm not meaning to be that way. Listen, let me tell you what happened. Maybe you can feel the truth. That's all I care about. That you feel it."

And so we started. She had researched everything completely, following the bear's removal from Alaska and the prosecution of the people involved, which led to the discovery of Doc's participation and the D.E.A. She would talk for hours and fall asleep while I tried to get it all down. She was very particular about the dialogue, remembering it exactly. She talked of truths as Anna and Adam told them and the conversations that Anna had with the horsemen as they made their way off the mountain.

She said they talked about the great scheme of life and things to come. They talked of servitude and devotion to fellow men. They spoke of the earth as a living entity and man's obligation to a living land. Micah said they spoke of the song Anna was to sing that would open the eyes of man. She said they spoke with great respect about Adam's life. She vowed to me that angels grieve.

I have never known a woman so deeply in love. I have never seen a love so complex in its form. I have never heard a story more unbelievable and yet I believe every word. She taught me about the truth, how to feel it, even when it was unclear. She taught me about being brave. She showed me about two worlds merging, both real, both full of hope.

There is a white moon over the mountain now, and that means something. Its wounding during that time has something do to with Adam, Micah and Anna, but there are some things I do not understand. She told me to pray about it and I would find the answer. She said that it amazes her now, how for thousands of years all societies are rooted in a belief of another reality, a spiritual reality with a Father who loves us and yet we are so reluctant to be brave and accept it. Live it. Embrace it. All faiths. All prayers. All people.

She left when I finished the manuscript. She cried

again and hugged my neck and the last I saw of her was the day she left with the dog in her truck. She smiled real big and told me not to worry, that she was finally happy. She said she was going to find Anna. She said she had to find her. I wish Micah well. I pray her a safe journey. We all do.

Micah, if you read this ... we are keeping the house up for your return. Since you left, there are sights on the mountain that would amaze you. Come home. We'll show you.

VIRGINIA

HANCOCK
COUNTY

TENNESSEE

JOHNSON
CITY

UNICOI
COUNTY

APPALACHIAN MOUNTAINS

NORTH CAROLINA

SOUTH CAROLINA